A Heartbeat Away

Amelia Marlowe

Copyright © 2024 by Amelia Marlowe

All rights reserved.

No portion of this book may be reproduced in any form without written permission from the publisher or author, except as permitted by U.S. copyright law.

Contents

1. Chapter 1 — 1
2. Chapter 2 — 11
3. Chapter 3 — 21
4. Chapter 4 — 35
5. Chapter 5 — 46
6. Chapter 6 — 58
7. Chapter 7 — 68
8. Chapter 8 — 84
9. Chapter 9 — 99
10. Chapter 10 — 113
11. Chapter 11 — 127
12. Chapter 12 — 141
13. Chapter 13 — 153
14. Chapter 14 — 172
15. Chapter 15 — 187

16.	Chapter 16	200
17.	Chapter 17	208
18.	Chapter 18	219
19.	Chapter 19	231
20.	Epilogue	241

Chapter 1

"If I die young, bury me in satin
    Lay me down on a bed of roses
Sink me in the river at dawn
Send me away with the words of a love song"

"Slow down, sweetheart!" A mother called as she chased a little girl through a flower field.

Laughter filled the air, a sweet innocent, musical laugh. Little legs propelled the young girl forward, long red locks flowing behind her. Until finally, she came to a stop and plopped down tiredly in the flower field.

The mother sat down next to the little girl, and her gaze washed over the child, memorizing the soft glow in her honey-brown eyes and the reddish flush to her cherub cheeks.

The field full of wildflowers was on the way to their house.

Year one, she'd stopped because the then one-year-old baby girl was fussy and needed a break; that's when she discovered that flowers calmed her down.

Year two, they'd stopped again, as she wanted to snap some pictures of the toddler in the flowers.

This was year three, and it was becoming a tradition, it seemed.

"Whats -a matter, mama?"

"I'm just a little sad, baby," she confessed.

"Why?"

"Don't you worry about it; it'll pass." She tapped the girl's little button nose. "Why don't you pick some flowers for your birthday?"

"Yay!" Full of smiles, she leaped up to do so, immediately taking off into a run.

"Stay where I can see you, London!"

"Beautiful," a girl murmured; one more flick of her wrist, and the pen did its magic.

"Loni, it's almost time for work!"

Her mother's voice pulled her from the zone she tended to get in when drawing or painting. The rose garden that filled the east side of the estate was Loni's favorite place to sit and paint. When it got close to her birthday, one bush of pink roses would bloom every year. She'd just finished drawing them and would paint them later.

Her dad told her it was her grandpa and grandma's way of saying happy birthday. They'd both passed away before she was born. Loni's full name was Leondra, after her grandpa Leonardo. He meant a lot to her family; he's what brought her parents together.

Clutching her sketchbook, Loni stood up, then sat right back down as a dizzy rush came over her. She'd been getting a lot of head rushes lately. Her mom had always said she should take more breaks when she was working, maybe she was right.

Once the feeling passed, the brunette stood again and headed towards the driveway, where her mom, Kit, and her sister, Lissa, were waiting. They both had their wavy coppery hair pulled up in loose buns, making them look like twins from a distance.

"Hurry up. I need a milkshake!" Lissa hollered as Loni got closer. The thirteen-year-old menace of a little sister was wearing Loni's brand-new sweater.

"Lissa! I just bought that," Loni complained. "It's huge on you anyway."

Lissa was petite like their mom, whereas Loni was tall like their dad, so Lissa only stood up to Loni's shoulder. The sweater she'd stolen hung down to her knobby little knees.

"I thought it was a sweater dress," Lissa said flippantly. "Looks better that way, see?"

Lissa started striking poses in the driveway, her blue eyes sparkling with amusement at Loni's annoyed expression.

"Lissa, enough. I told you to ask before wearing your sister's clothes," Kit scolded as she unlocked the car. "Loni, we don't have three hours for her to change. I'll get you a new sweater if she ruins it."

"Fine," Loni relented as she climbed in. "Why the hurry anyway?"

"I have five hundred cupcakes to make for your birthday party this Friday." Kit was only slightly exaggerating. Maybe twenty or thirty people would be at her party, but she always made way too much.

They pulled out of the long driveway of their estate. They had a massive house on a large plot of land, and a smaller guest house sat behind it, where her aunt, uncle, and cousins lived when they weren't traveling. They'd be back for Loni's birthday soon.

It was a five-minute drive to Leo's E Famiglia, her family's restaurant. Everyone in town just called it Leo's. Loni had taken up a part-time job there when school ended last week, helping her dad, Luca, in the kitchen. She loved cooking; it was a lot of fun, mostly because got to she spend so much time with her dad.

Kit parked, and Lissa raced inside and Kit and Loni were right behind her.

It was a beautiful restaurant, big and spacious with hardwood floors; the walls were decorated with photos of food and wine, some Loni even painted herself.

As usual, Lissa went right over to the jukebox, and Kit headed back into the kitchen.

"Hey Loni!"

Loni looked over and smiled at a few of her school friends sitting at a table. Leo's was a popular spot for the high school kids during the summer.

"You working today, or can you join us?" Andrea, her best friend, asked as she tucked her chocolate hair behind her ear.

"Working," Loni answered. "You're all coming to my birthday party Friday, right?"

"Of course!"

"Can't wait!"

"Are you inviting, Manny?" Andrea motioned to the busboy her dad had hired that summer. Manny was new in town, and no one knew much about him besides that he was quiet. Not to mention super cute with his olive hued tanned skin, dark hair, and emerald green eyes.

He was cleaning a table and looked up when Loni looked over.

He gave her a sweet smile that instantly made her heart speed up and caused little flutters in her belly. She smiled back and offered a little wave.

Why are you waving at him? She asked herself. Ugh. She was so bad at this flirting stuff.

"He so likes you. Just ask him," Andrea insisted.

"Maybe," Loni said nervously; the very idea was causing her heart to nearly thunder in her chest.

Not nearly... it was. Why was her heart beating this fast? Was this normal? Are boys supposed to make you think you're going to die?

"There's the cutest sous chef in the world," Luca declared loudly as he walked out of the kitchen.

Her friends all giggled at that; most of them had a crush on her dad, well, all of them. Loni took a few deep breaths to calm her heart and then hustled over to her dad.

"Dad, that was so embarrassing," she complained.

"Good, I like keeping you nice and mortified."

"What? Why?"

"It's a revenge thing."

"Revenge for what? I don't do anything wrong." Loni folded her arms over her chest and pursed her lips.

"Christ, you look just like your mom when you do that," Luca said with a shake of his head.

Even though Loni had light brown hair and was tall like her dad, her facial features were very similar to her mom's, they had the same amber doe-like eyes, pouty lips, and cheeks that blushed far too easily. Lissa, on the other hand, had her mom's red hair, small stature, but her dad's bright blue eyes, and little smirk. Her mom always loved to say how the girls were a perfect mix of them both.

"And it's revenge for these." Luca ran his hand through his shaggy hair, which was beginning to show streaks of gray.

"Hey, daddio, I need a milkshake!" Lissa yelled out. "Strawberry, puleasssse!"

Luca cringed when his gaze found his younger daughter. "Lissa, how many times do I have to- Get off the damn table!"

Loni turned around to see Lissa on top of one of the big rounds dancing in the center as one of her favorite boy bands played in the background.

"But this is my jam!" Lissa did a little spin and then jumped down.

"She's the one who gives you grey hairs," Loni told Luca with a roll of her eyes.

Manny walked by then with a bus tub, and for a second, their gazes locked. Her lips lifted in a nervous smile, and just as he was about to return it, he walked right into the bar.

"Oof," Manny grunted.

"Manny, are you okay!?" Loni asked worriedly as she heard her dad stifle a laugh.

"I'm fine," he looked embarrassed as he quickly ducked back into the kitchen after that.

"No.." Luca watched Manny disappear and then ruffled Loni's hair. "It's you."

"That milkshake isn't going to make itself!" Lissa sang out.

"Actually, it's both of you," Luca muttered as he ducked behind the bar.

Lunch was pretty slow, so Luca let Loni do most of the cooking herself while he helped Kit with the cupcakes in the back of the kitchen.

"You got a little something right here," she heard her dad say as her mom squealed.

"Luca! Stop! I'll be washing frosting out of my hair all night!" Kit mock scolded him.

"I can help with that," Luca said in a low tone, and Loni groaned out loud.

"Your kid is still in here!" She reminded them but they ignored her as her mom giggled at something her dad whispered to her.

"Gross! I'll go wait for you out front, mom," Loni said wisely.

They'd probably start making out soon. They were seriously disgusting, but secretly she did love how much her parents adored each other. She dreamed of a love just like that someday.

She headed out front and saw most everyone was gone. Her sister was sitting at a table playing games on her iPad, and one other table remained.

Manny was filling a bus tub with dishes at the bar and looked up when Loni stepped out.

"Hey, uh.. lunch seemed to go good," he offered. "You're a good cook like your dad."

"Yeah? Thanks," she smiled as she stepped a little closer. That fluttery feeling was back, but at least her heart wasn't beating out of her chest this time.

"Are you going to be a chef like him someday?"

"Maybe," Loni said, "but I also love painting."

"You do?"

"Yeah, I did those," she gestured to a few of the wall hangings her dad so proudly displayed of her art.

"Whoa! Those are great. You are super talented!" Manny exclaimed.

"They're okay." A bashful blush spread over her cheeks. "I prefer painting flowers. I love flowers, especially roses."

"I'd love to see more of what you painted."

"Really? Maybe, I could bring my sketchbook in some time."

"Yeah! You should."

"So, um. I don't know if you heard it's my birthday on Friday," Loni started, and then her heart begun to race.. her palms were also all sweaty, so she ran them against the side of her jeans.

"I did, Luca said the staff is off that day since it's here."

"Would you... I mean, if you want to come, you can." Loni was pretty sure her face was beet red at this point.

"Sure, I'd love to," he smiled shyly.

"Great!" She smiled back at him, hoping he didn't hear how loud her heart was racing "Everyone is coming by around five, I think."

"Okay, I'll see you then," he ran a hand through his dark locks.

Luca coughed from behind them, and Manny nearly jumped a foot.

"Uh, I better back these dishes to the kitchen," Manny's eyes shifted from her to Luca, and then he ran off.

"Dad!" Loni complained as she whirled around to face him.

"I don't recall saying you could date," Luca raised an eyebrow as Kit stepped out behind him.

"Mom!" Loni looked at Kit for help. "I'm going to be sixteen!"

"Luca. She's old enough to date," Kit said, looking amused as she squeezed his shoulder.

"We don't know a thing about that kid!" Luca complained.

"Just the other day, you told me what a huge help he is here," Kit pointed out. "I think your exact words were, that Manny is a good kid."

"That doesn't mean he gets to date my daughter!"

"Luca..." Kit said warningly.

"It's not even a date. I invited him to my party. Everyone will be there watching us, I'm sure." Loni said irritably.

"Between dad, uncle Andre, and your grandpa, that's a pretty safe bet," Kit agreed. "Luca, do I need sing, Let it Go?"

"Fine, since we'll all be there, but no date -dates yet. Not until we sit down and go over the rules," Luca said sternly.

"Yeah, like no kissing!" Lissa had joined them and started making kissy faces. "Oh, Manny! You're so cute!"

"Lissa, knock it off!" a mortified Loni exclaimed.

Thankfully Manny was still in the kitchen. Luca and Kit both started cracking up, only infuriating Loni further.

"I'll be in the car," Loni huffed as she stormed off.

The door fell shut behind her as Loni walked out the parking lot, she was excited to text Andrea and tell her. Asking Manny to her party was way easier than she'd thought it would be.

So why was her heart still beating like a drum?

Chapter 2

"Lord, make me a rainbow. I'll shine down on my mother. She'll know I'm safe with you when she stands under my colors."

"Mama, look!" Wide eyes were full of excitement as they looked ahead. "Red flowers!"

"Those are roses," she told her little girl as they walked the field, little hand held firmly in hers.

It was year five, and this trip to the flower field had become something they both looked forward to all year. Her husband's new job at the hospital forced them to move away from the little house near the flowery field after the third year, but still, mom and daughter made a trip out there to honor the tradition.

"Can we pick some?"

"Not these, London. They have thorns."

"Oh," a frown took over her little face.

"Don't be sad. Some flowers are only meant to be looked at. We can admire them just how they are without ever disturbing them. Let them grow, bloom and die all on their own." Her own words caused sadness to wash over her.

The words fell short on the little girl's ears, though, as she was too busy admiring the red roses.

"What if we take some pictures of you with the roses?"

"Okay, mama!" The little girl stood before the bush and beamed a big bright smile.

Laughter fell from the mother's lips, her sadness momentarily forgotten. "Give me a minute to get my camera phone out, silly girl."

Little London loved posing, and they took several photos that day.

Then they huddled together in the field and scrolled through them.

Photos, she could never take enough of her children. Her husband teased her and liked to call her the paparazzi. He didn't understand why they meant so much to her.

"Mama, when we get home I'm gonna color the flowers!" London broke up her melancholy thoughts with her cheerful voice.

"Well, that sounds like a great idea, sweetheart. We'll get you some fresh crayons and blank paper on the way to pick up your cake."

"Yay!" She ran to the middle of the field again and began spinning around, her red locks flying all over, covering her face.

So much joy.

A tear slipped down the mother's cheek as she watched.

Thursday evening was calm at the Donato house as they waited for her aunt, uncle, and cousins to arrive. They hadn't been back for over a year, and Loni was so touched they were coming for her birthday.

The house was spacious, with grey wood floors, bright white walls, and stone trim. It also had enormous windows that gave it a lot of light. It had a great open layout with lots of space for the kitchen and living room. A large staircase sat in the center of the living room and led to Loni and Lissa's bedrooms and a few guest rooms.

Their parent's room sat downstairs off the living room on the main floor, and a small office sat near the kitchen.

Loni lounged on the couch with Kit watching television, while Luca prepared dinner. Lissa was outside playing on the little jungle gym her dad built for them several years ago.

Chaos in the form of her two eight-year-old twin cousins, Ruthie and Len, broke up the peace when they both came running into the house without warning.

"We're here!" Len screamed; he'd gotten taller but was a skinny little thing. Blonde locks were hanging in his green eyes.

"Happy birthday, Loni!" Ruthie yelled even louder. She was even tinier than Len, and her hair was a mess of blonde curls.

"Aren't you two full of energy," Kit laughed as she stood to greet them, giving them each a kiss on the head.

"We can see you; you don't have to yell," Luca chuckled.

"Uncle Luca!" Ruthie was all smiles as she started running to him.

"Hi, Ruthie!" Luca lifted her in the air as she cheered, he gave her a kiss on her cheek and she giggled. Len raced over next as Luca put Ruthie down scoop him up for a hug.

Their old golden retriever Lucky came bounding down the stairs to see what the excitement was all about.

"Lucky!" Len raced over and started playing with him, getting the dog all riled up while Ruthie laughed gleefully.

"Go easy on him. He's getting old," Loni warned just as her uncle Andre and aunt Carly walked in.

"You and me both, Lucky," Andre said as he patted the dogs head.

"Why don't you two take the dog outside and see Lissa?" Kit suggested. "she's in the backyard."

The two blonde twins bounded out the back door with Lucky in tow. He'd be exhausted tonight.

"Loni!" Carly clasped Loni's hands in hers. "Girl, you are flipping gorgeous. Look at you! Those long legs, and those, lips, I can't stop staring at you, you should be a model, seriously"

"Settle down, she's not modeling" Luca growled, and Andre laughed.

"Did you just growl?" Andre teased as he walked into the kitchen to see what Luca was cooking.

"She could be a model," Kit said proudly. "She's so tall and those cheekbones. Just like her dad."

"Everybody stop!" Loni was blushing hard.

"And she's bashful. Stay this sweet okay," Carly kissed her cheek. "Don't ever change."

If anyone could be a model, it was her aunt Carly. She was beautiful, with curly blonde hair, sparkling blue eyes, and a figure to die for. She was always dressed up in the most fashionable clothes too.

Her uncle Andre was much more casual looking; he kept his light brown hair cut short and usually wore jeans and a tee shirt or a flannel.

Her mom told her he used to be very formal and conservative, but had loosened up a lot when he and Carly started to travel. Loni and Lissa loved hearing stories and seeing photos of all the places they'd go.

"So, Loni, have you met any boys you like yet?" Carly asked teasingly as she sat down at the table and Kit joined her." or girls, I didn't mean to assume."

"Boys and just one boy," Loni blushed harder than ever.

"Manny," Kit said with a cheeky grin. "He's adorable and so shy."

"Ah! Andre was shy!" Carly cheered happily. "Is he sweet? What does he look like? Tell me more!"

"There are just friends, and that's all they're going to be until Loni is eighteen," Luca spoke up from the kitchen, causing Loni to glare at him.

"Dad, eighteen? That's silly!"

"You're right, let's make it closer to twenty."

"Luca!" Kit shot him a look as Andre cracked up laughing.

"Not funny, little brother."

"Have you and Stone given him the poison yet?" Andre asked, and a smirk took over her dad's features.

"That's an idea."

"The what?" Loni frowned in confusion. "That sounds bad. Dad, you better not!"

"He won't," Kit said and then looked at Luca. "I told you and my dad that was banned a long time ago. You are not testing our daughter's dates with it."

"What is it?" Loni asked curiously. Her grandpa Stone was funny; he drank and smoked a lot. A lot. But he was super fun. Probably the funniest guy she'd ever known.

"It's a horrible liquor concoction your grandpa put together."

"And he tested your boyfriends with it?" Loni asked.

"I'm the only one that passed," Luca bragged as he came to set the pasta he'd made down at the table.

"Really?" Loni asked curiously.

"The guy before me almost died from it."

"What?" Loni's eyes nearly popped out of her head. "I don't want you to give that to Manny then!"

"He won't," Kit said with a steely look at Luca.

"She's right, Loni. I won't," Luca said. "You want to know why?"

"Why?" Loni asked.

"Because I don't want you with anyone that can drink that shit," Luca explained. "Don't end up with a mini-me."

"Well, someone that loves her like you love, would make me happy, but not someone that drinks the way you used to," Kit mused. "...and, I think one mini-Luca in the family is more then enough."

"Maybe we should go into hiding when Lissa starts dating?" Luca suggested. "I'm already anticipating the angry parents she'll be sending to our door."

"That's probably a good idea," Kit agreed.

"We're still going to test this Manny out, though," Andre pointed out. "With a bunch of questions. Got to make sure he's good enough."

"Should we take him into the walk-in pantry and drill him?" Luca asked, and Andre nodded in agreement.

"Great idea," Andre said, "small space so he can't get away."

"You the good cop, and I'm the bad cop then?" Luca asked as he smirked at Loni's horrified glare.

"Nah, let's both be bad cops; see how much we can make him sweat."

"Andre," Carly laughed. "Be nice to the boy; he's shy like you were."

"It's good practice for when Ruthie dates," Luca pointed out.

"Mom! Don't let them do this!" Loni looked at Kit for help.

"Sorry, honey," Kit said with a smile. "I can stop the poison, but I can't stop them from protecting you."

"Dad be nice, please," Loni begged.

"Oh, relax, pumpkin," Luca patted her head affectionately. "I like Manny. I plan to chat with him, but not at your birthday, okay?"

Relief washed over her, well, momentary relief anyhow. At least she bought some time before her dad scared Manny away.

"He's a good guy, dad," Loni assured him.

"No one's good enough for my baby girl," Luca said with a sad smile.

"Oh, dad," she hugged him and he squeezed her tightly.

"Stop growing up so fast," he said as he kissed her head.

"Is it time for dinner yet?" Lissa and the twins came running back in. "We're starving!"

"As soon as you set the table," Luca directed.

"Why can't Loni set the table?" Lissa whined.

"Because she worked today, and she always sets the table. Now stop arguing with me and move your little legs," Luca demanded.

"Fiiiiiiine," Lissa groaned.

She stomped into the kitchen as if he asked her to scrub the entire house from top to bottom.

"Yeah, she's you," Andre noted.

"Yup," Luca agreed, he still had Loni tucked under his arm and affectionately patted her head. "This one is dad's gift. That one is dad's revenge."

"Luca!" Kit exclaimed, but she laughed anyway.

Later that night, Loni woke up on the couch with Lucky's head on her lap. Their parents had popped in a movie for them after dinner.

Lissa was sprawled across the recliner, snoring, Len was on the floor on an air mattress her mom had brought out, and Ruthie was on the other end of the couch.

Ruthie woke as Lucky got up with Loni shaking the couch. Her cousin yawned as brushed her long blonde locks from her face.

"Sorry, I didn't mean to wake you," Loni whispered. "I'm going to head up to bed. You can have the whole couch."

"Okay, Loni," she yawned again.

"You warm enough?" Loni asked as she stood up.

"I'm-"

She didn't register the answer as the room began to spin, and black dots filled her vision.

"Loni!"

A cry from Ruthie caught Loni's attention, and she sat up from the floor.

Her head began to clear, but she frowned. She fell? Did she black out for a second? This was worse then the head rushes she'd been getting when she was too focused on panting.

It must just be a head rush from watching television in the dark, she told herself. No big deal, just tired that's all.

Ruthie was running to her, and Loni sat up quickly to comfort her worried cousin.

"I'm okay, Ruthie. Just tripped is all."

"I'm gonna go get uncle Luca," Ruthie said with a frown.

"No, don't!" Loni stopped her by gently grabbing her arm.

He'd make her stay home and rest tomorrow if he thought she was getting sick. She couldn't risk him canceling her party. All her friends were going to be there, not to mention Manny.

"But Loni-" Ruthie's blue eyes were full of worry.

"I'm fine, Ruthie," Loni assured the little girl as she stood. "See. All better."

"But you fell down.."

"It was no big deal, don't tell my parents. They'll worry for no reason."

"Okay," Ruthie was returning to the couch to lie down, but her face was still full of worry.

"Are you sure you're okay, Loni?" Ruthie asked after Loni kissed her forehead and pulled the blanket over her.

"Of course I'm okay," Loni promised. "Now get some sleep. It's a big day tomorrow."

An uneasy feeling came over Loni she she headed upstairs with Lucky in tow. She did her best to ignore it, but it lingered.

Chapter 3

Loni woke the next day to her bed bouncing as Lissa jumped on it.

"Happy Birthday!" The tiny redhead cheered as Loni looked up.

"Lissa, what time is it?" Loni yawned; she was exhausted. Had she slept at all last night?

"It's time for your birthday; that's what time it is! Dad made the birthday pancakes!"

A favorite Donato tradition was pancakes for birthday breakfasts, not just any pancakes either, chocolate chip, homemade from scratch.

"Loni Boni Fo Foni Fe Fie Fo Foni Loni!" Lissa sang out loud as she jumped up and down until finally, Loni sat up, giggling at her little sister's antics.

"I'm up, I'm up," Loni groaned in an amused tone. "Will you stop jumping on my bed now?"

Lissa responded by jumping down to Loni's soft carpeted floor.

"Where is Lucky?"

"He came down a while ago; you slept so late," Lissa informed her.

"Really?" Loni yawned; then why was she still so tired?

"Yeah, dad told me to come to get you before the pancakes get too cold." Lissa said as she headed out, "so hurry up and come down!"

Loni slowly swung her legs over the side of the bed. Last night's fall still haunted her; luckily no head rush this time. She slipped a sweatshirt she'd stolen from her dad over her pajamas; it was big, warm, and comforting.

As she made her way downstairs, she saw that everyone was already sitting at the table, and two huge plates of pancakes sat in the center. When she reached the bottom, a lot of commotion happened at once.

"There's the birthday girl!" Luca cheered as he flashed her a grin.

"Happy birthday, sweet sixteen," her mom smiled, patting the seat next to her as Loni walked over to it and sat down.

"Happy birthday, Loni!" Uncle Andre greeted her.

"Hurry up and eat, so we can. These chocolate chip pancakes are driving me crazy!" Lissa begged.

The twins started to sing happy birthday as Aunt Carly explained that singing would be later.

"Thanks, everyone," Loni smiled and blushed from the attention as she sat down.

Luca filled a plate of pancakes and slid them over to her. They looked amazing, big and fluffy, topped with a dollop of butter and homemade whipped cream, but she didn't really feel hungry for them.

Everyone else was digging in and giving lots of compliments to her proud dad.

"Honey, are you feeling okay? You haven't touched your pancakes," Kit noted.

"I'm just not that hungry," Loni confessed, hoping her dad's feelings wouldn't be hurt. "My stomach feels a little funny."

"Are you getting sick?" Luca looked up worriedly, as did Kit.

"I don't think so; it feels kind of fluttery or something," Loni explained the anxious feeling.

"Sounds like you're nervous about your party," Carly suggested.

"Because Manny is going to be there," Lissa teased, and Loni stuck her tongue out at her.

"You sure you're okay?" Kit asked as her gaze washed over Loni carefully.

"Fine, mom," Loni assured her. "I think Aunt Carly is right; I've been feeling more nervous the closer the party gets."

"You have nothing to be worried about, pumpkin," Luca reached over and squeezed her shoulder. "Everyone's going to have a blast; all you have to do is show up and have fun."

"Thanks, dad," Loni offered a smile; usually, he could quickly ease her mind, but today she still had an uneasy feeling bugging her. She brushed it aside as she sat and listened to her family chat over breakfast.

The rest of the day, Loni lounged around reading and napped a little off and on until it was time to get dressed for her party. She felt a lot better after taking it easy all day.

Her mom helped her pick a pink and white flowery dress for her birthday dress, and she wore a white cardigan over it. Aunt Carly helped her curl her hair into soft saves, and Kit surprised her with a makeup set as an early birthday present.

They showed her how to do her eyeliner and blush, and when they were all done, she was stunned at how grown up she looked. So was her mom as she started crying, and Loni quickly embraced her.

"Oh, mom, don't cry!"

"You're just growing up so fast," Kit sniffled. "Will you stop it!"

"Kit, don't do that, or I'll start," Carly cried.

"Both of you, stop!" Loni giggled, "we'll ruin all our make-up."

"She's so smart," Kit pulled her into a hug and kissed the top of her head. "I love you, Leondra."

"Love you, mom," Loni let the warm feeling of her mom's love wash over her as they hugged.

"Can I wear makeup too?" Lissa came bouncing in, wearing a shiny and sparkling red dress that was loose on her small frame; with it, she had her red cowboy boots on.

"Oh, Lissa, where did you find that dress," Kit laughed as she took in her younger daughter, who was already dabbing blush heavily on her cheeks.

"Aha, the red dress!" Carly added, invoking Loni's curiosity.

"It was in the back of your closet," Lissa did a little shimmy. "I like it."

"You should. It's why you exist," Carly said with a short laugh.

"Carly!" Kit exclaimed.

"Huh?" Loni looked at Kit for clarification, but she just shook her head.

"You don't want to know," Carly offered through her laughter.

"You ladies all almost ready?" Came her dad's impatient call from downstairs.

Lissa picked up a tube of lipstick and popped the top off. "Almost!"

"Don't ruin all my new makeup," Loni warned her.

"I'll help her with it; head on down, we'll be right behind you," Kit said as she took the lipstick from Lissa.

As Loni headed downstairs, her Uncle Andre made a dramatic whistling sound that made her blush, and her dad looked proud in his teary blue eyes.

"Look at you, all grown up," Luca said with a sad smile as she reached the bottom step. "You look beautiful, birthday girl."

"Thanks, dad," Loni smiled as he embraced her.

"I love you, pumpkin."

"Love, you too, dad," she kissed his cheek.

She could see him wiping at his eyes as they parted, and she gave him a playful shove.

"Will you all stop acting like I'm getting married or something? I'm just turning sixteen."

"Yeah, chill out, daddio," Lissa called out as she danced and shimmied her way down the stairs with Kit and Carly behind her.

Luca studied her momentarily and then tipped his head over to Kit with a chuckle. "Kit Kat, is that the casino dress?"

"Yup. I have no idea how she found it, babe," Kit said with a short laugh.

"Oh, that takes me back," her dad smiled fondly as he made googly eyes at her mom, who blushed furiously under his stare. Imagine that, still blushing at him after all these years. They were so cute, gross but cute.

"Don't I look pretty, daddy?" Lissa asked as she did a spin once she reached the bottom.

"Gorgeous, shorty" he picked her up and spun her around. "will you save a dance for your old man tonight?"

"I suppose," Lissa said in a sing-song voice.

"I guess we better figure out who is riding with who," Luca commented as he put Lissa down.

He gave Kit a little wink, and she grinned back at him.

"Well, two cars would be the easiest, don't you think?" Kit asked in a coy tone.

"Sure would," Luca said slowly, "But what two cars?"

"Why are you guys being all weird?" Loni looked from one to the other. "We can all go in mom's van, and Uncle Andre, Aunt Carly, and their kids will go in their car."

"That could work," Andre was biting back a grin, and Carly nudged him.

"Okay, what's going on?" Loni demanded to know.

"Better go outside and see for yourself," Kit nudged her with a grin.

Shooting one more questioning look towards them, Loni felt her heart racing with anticipation. Could it be? They had been practicing all spring, but her dad was so protective, no way.

He wouldn't have gotten her a...

"A car!" Loni screamed when she opened the door, and her eyes landed on the shiny red civic with a big bow on top of it. "This is mine?"

"It's yours, pumpkin," Luca said as her mom added, "happy birthday."

"Thank you, thank you so much!" Squealing with excitement, Loni raced towards both of them, and they enveloped her in a huge group hug., Meanwhile, Lissa went racing over to the car and started dancing near it.

"We got a car! We got a car!" Lissa was singing as she spun around.

"I got a car!" Loni whirled around to correct her.

"There are some rules that go along with this car," Luca warned as Loni raced to get a better look.

"But we can go over those tomorrow; tonight, why don't you drive me, dad, and Lissa to your party?" Kit suggested, and Loni's eyes lit up with excitement and happiness.

"Best birthday ever!" Loni exclaimed as Luca tossed her the keys.

The excitement over the car had Loni's heart racing as she carefully drove to Leo's; her dad sat in the passenger's seat next to her, carefully watching as she drove.

"You're white-knuckling the wheel; loosen up a little," Luca guided her.

"Don't be nervous, honey," Kit added from the back, "you're doing great. Just take a few breaths."

She did just that in and out, in and out, but that nervous fluttery feeling in her belly was coming back in a hurry.

"Can I drive home?" Lissa asked.

"Sure," Luca quipped.

"Really!" Lissa's eyes lit up as both Kit and Loni frowned.

"Really, in three years."

"Dad," she groaned at that and sulked in her seat.

As she pulled into the parking lot, she parked next to her grandpa Stone just as he exited his truck. He was dressed down like usual in torn-up jeans and a flannel, his gray hair tucked under a baseball cap. He beamed a big proud smile when he saw that Loni was driving.

"Wow! Look at that, your own car!" Stone whistled as he ran a hand over it. "she's nice."

"Hi, Grandpa!" Loni raced over to hug him. "isn't it nice?"

"Looks great, birthday girl," Stone squeezed her. "Now I can call you when I need a sober cab."

"Ha-ha," Luca said dryly. "She's not driving after dark, so day drink then."

"Oh, I do," Stone joked to which Kit raised an eyebrow.

"I'm kidding, I'm a day stoner and night drinker," he assured her.

"Hiya, Grandpa!" Lissa bounded into his arms, and he scooped her up.

"Did you get shorter since I last saw ya?" Stone asked as he set her down, and she crinkled her nose at him.

"No! but you did!"

"I did not!" He gasped as if offended.

"Yup cause smoking makes you shrink," Lissa informed him.

"Is that so?" Stone looked at Luca with an amused grin.

"That's what I heard," Luca confirmed. "among other bad things."

"Aha I see. Your dad's right, I used to be almost eight feet tall."

"That's not true," Lissa rolled her eyes and scoffed. "But the last thing I need is any shrinking."

"I think you mean stunt your growth..." Loni commented but Lissa just shrugged.

Stone patted Lissa's head. "What's with the dress?"

"It's moms," Lissa twirled around in circles. "Let's go inside and dance!"

Lissa led the way into the restaurant, and Loni was excited to see all her friends had already arrived; some were chatting at the jukebox, and a few were seated at different tables. The restaurant was beautifully decorated with many flowers, mostly roses, a big happy birthday banner, and lots of balloons.

"Happy birthday Loni!" Andrea called from a table with a handful of her other friends, and Loni waved at them.

"Go ahead, and join your friends, honey," Kit said, "I'm going to wait for Carly, Andre, and the kids."

"I'm going to go check on the food," Luca ruffled her hair and then darted off to the kitchen.

Loni headed toward Andrea and her friends. They made room for her to sit down and join them.

"I love your dress," Andrea enthused.

"You look so pretty!" Kelly added.

"I got a car for my birthday!" Loni couldn't help but squeal in excitement, still stunned by it.

"Oh my god, your dad is literally the best," Andrea gushed.

"Well, my mom probably talked him into it," Loni pointed out.

"Truth, she's the best, too," Andrea said as she stood from the booth, "let's go see the car!"

She was dressed in a pink and black dress with skyscraper heels, her dark brown hair in a curly bun. Andrea and Loni had been friends for as long as she could remember, but Andrea had changed over the last few years. She used to be very bookish and quiet, and most of their days were spent with Loni painting while Andrea read a book, but over the last year, shopping, cheerleading, and hanging out with friends and stuff had taken precedence over Andrea's old hobbies. Andrea's new friends were nice enough to Loni, but she didn't feel like she fully clicked with any of them.

"Hold that thought," Loni said as the familiar cute boy entered the door. "Manny is here."

"ooooh," Kelly teased while the rest of the girls giggled.

"Stop," Loni hushed them as her cheeks flushed bright red.

She walked over to Manny, and he froze as his eyes locked on hers. His mouth was slightly open, and his eyes were wide as they took her in; she felt her cheeks flushing hard. He looked more dressed up than she'd ever seen him; he wore a pair of dark blue jeans that could be new and a nice button-down black shirt. His dark hair was combed straight. He was holding a gift bag in his hand.

"Hi, Manny," she finally spoke, and her voice came out all high-pitched.

"I'm glad you came." She added, sounding a little more normal.

"Uh yeah, me too... " Hi," he muttered sheepishly, "er, um, happy birthday."

"Thanks," she giggled nervously; somehow, his being all sky and awkward made her feel better.

"I sound like an idiot, don't I?" He asked with a pitiful look in his green eyes.

"No!" Loni couldn't help but laugh. "Not anymore, then I do."

The jukebox began playing, and music filled the air behind them; she led him further inside and found an empty table for the two of them to sit at.

"Happy birthday," he said, handing her the gift bag he'd carried in.

"Manny! You didn't have to do this!" She exclaimed as she pulled it closer.

"It's nothing, really," he shrugged.

She opened the bag and gasped as she pulled out a brand-new sketchbook and charcoal pencils.

"You said you liked drawing and painting; I didn't know what to get for paint, but I figured you could use these?"

"Oh, I can, and I will. I wear out my stuff fast; this is great, thank you!"

"Yeah, you really like it?"

"I do," she flashed him a smile, and he smiled back, looking less nervous himself now as well.

"I think it's cool that you draw and cook," Manny said. "Most kids I know our age only watch TV or shop."

"Well, I do that too," Loni laughed. "What about you? What do you do when you're not working?"

"I used to play the guitar some, sing a little," he admitted.

"Really! That's so cool," Loni enthused. "You don't anymore, though?"

"I uh... had to sell my guitar last year."

"Sell it?" she frowned, "why?"

"It's kind of a long story," he looked at her carefully. "But don't worry about all that; I'll have a new one someday."

She wondered why he'd had to sell it. Couldn't he have asked his parents for money? She wanted to ask more but didn't want to seem nosy or rude. She glanced at her new sketchbook and felt a stab of guilt. Did that present set him back from getting a new guitar?

"You look pretty tonight," he blurted out, looking sheepish. "I mean, you always look pretty, but.. um, that dress is nice."

"Thank you," she smiled as her cheeks flamed red. "You look really good too."

Really good? She cringed, but he was beaming, so maybe it wasn't so terrible after all.

"Do you want to dance?" he asked, and she glanced over to see many teenagers, including her little sister, had made their way to the center of the room and were dancing to a fast song.

"Sure!"

He took her hand in his as they started to walk to the dance floor, giving her a tingle in her whole body; she glanced over to see her mom and Carly watching. Her mom winked and Carly gave her a thumbs up.

She rolled her eyes and pulled Manny further from their eyeshot to the middle of the floor. He was moving awkwardly, shifting from foot to foot, and she wasn't much better. Finally, she started loosening up a little when Lissa spun past them all crazy-like.

Manny laughed as Loni spun around more dramatically, smiling, and laughing as she started having more fun, the nerves sliding away.

Manny started loosening up too, and soon he clasped her hands, and they started spinning together; it was like everyone in the room disappeared except for them. She didn't even care how silly they probably both looked as they danced badly whilst holding hands.

They were quickly getting out of breath from the fast movements and the laughing. The song stopped, and they stood facing each other, their eyes locked. His eyes nearly seemed to sparkle as they looked at her, and she was sure hers were the same. The only trouble was that her heart was still racing from that dance. She had trouble catching her breath, even as Manny's breathing regulated.

His eyes changed from the cute look he'd been giving her to one of concern as he took a step closer. "Loni? Are you okay?"

She gasped as she struggled to breathe, shaking her head in panic.

"Are you choking on something?" he came closer and patted her back hard, and she coughed, a horrible hacking sound came out of her, and several teens turned to look at her in the same horrified way Manny was.

She couldn't focus on that, though, because she was still breathing so raggedly, and on top of that, she was suddenly very dizzy; the entire room was spinning.

"Loni?!"

"Get my dad..." was the last thing she gasped out before everything went black.

Chapter 4

"Life ain't always what you think ought to be, no. Ain't even gray when she buries her baby. The sharp knife of a short life."

By year seven, the field of flowers had an abundance of purple flowers, and they'd taken over most of the area. Little London was plopped down in the middle of them, her purple crayon down to a nub as she colored the area.

She had shown quite a talent for art and drawing over the last few years. Where this creative talent came from was a mystery.

"That looks beautiful, sweetheart," the mother encouraged.

"Thank you, mama," London's soft brown eyes were focused on the paper as she drew. "I'm going to be a drawer when I grow up."

"It's called an artist."

"Artist," London corrected herself; she was maturing so quickly.

A lump formed in the mother's throat as she stared into the distance.

"Mama?"

She turned to find her little girl peering at her with curious eyes.

"What is it, sweetheart?"

"Why are you sad?"

"I'm not sad. Don't you worry about mama." She tapped her little button nose, but the worried look didn't fade from London's eyes; her eyebrows furrowed, and her little lips twisted into a pout.

"But you always seem sad here, and it's my favorite spot in the world."

"This is my favorite spot in the world too. I get a little sad on you and your brother's birthdays," the mother confessed.

"But why?"

"Because it's hard to see you two growing up."

The answer didn't seem to satisfy young London. It felt as if her eyes were searching her mother for the truth as if she could pull it out of her soul.

"I think we ought to get going, sweetheart. We still need to get the house ready for your birthday party."

"Is daddy going to be there?"

"He's going to try as best as he can," was all she could offer as a promise. "You know how busy daddy can get; his patients need him."

"Cause they are very sick?"

"That's right."

"I hope daddy can make them all better."

"My sweet, sweet girl."

When Kit Donato woke up on Friday morning, sixteen felt like so many years. It made her feel old to think her oldest daughter was that age. Looking at Loni with a face full of makeup and a pretty dress, she thought, my girl is so mature, so beautiful.

Then later, Kit watched Loni confidently pull Manny to the dance floor with a big bright smile and a happy glint in her eyes, and she thought, she's all grown up.

...And then in the blink of an eye it all changed

Kit felt it before she knew it. It was like a cold shock that jolted her entire body; she stood and screamed right before the rest of the crowd did.

"Kit, what's"-

"call nine-one-one," Kit shouted at Carly, and then she lunged forward.

She couldn't see a thing as she made her way through the crowd of teenagers; she didn't have to, though; she just knew.

Something was wrong; something was very, very wrong.

Even though she knew this, when she finally got to the center of the room and saw Loni crumbled up in Manny's arms, she dropped to her knees in shock.

"Loni!" A guttural scream left her throat, and then the room went radio silent.

Kit saw Luca running; she'd never seen him run that fast. Manny looked pale and terrified as he handed Loni to Luca. Why was the room so silent? Why couldn't Kit speak or move? Manny's lips moved fast, and Luca lowered Loni to the ground.

An ambulance. Did Carly call an ambulance?

Luca looked at his wife and yelled something, but in her fog, she couldn't hear him. She wanted to stand, but couldn't make her legs work, but then she felt someone lifting her, her dad maybe?

"Cricket! I need you!" Luca's voice lifted the fog and everyone else's all came back at once and it was like a roar of sound.

Without wasting another second, Kit was up and racing toward Luca; he'd already started performing CPR on Loni. Kit knew CPR from her short stint in nursing school and ensured Luca knew it too, after they had kids. She'd hoped they'd never need to know it, but was glad they did. She knelt beside her husband to assist him.

As Luca pressed down on Loni's chest, tears ran down Kit's face, but she refused to think about anything but getting their daughter to breathe again. Kit tilted Loni's chin and breathed life into her mouth.

Loni's chest rose as it filled with air, and she coughed and sputtered as she exhaled. Loni gasped, and Kit sat her up, patting her back until the ragged breaths turned into a horrible wet cough.

She then helped Loni tilt her head down and spit out, a lot of fluid. When Loni sat back up, she was red-faced and panting but finally breathing again.

Kit looked up and was thankful to see her dad shooing the kids away as the medical team arrived.

Loni was trying to say something, but Kit shushed and held her close, kissing her head. "Don't talk; just breathe, baby. Just breathe."

Luca was trembling beside them, his face as pale as she'd ever seen, his blue eyes stricken with the same cold fear that gripped Kit's heart.

"What happened?" The paramedic asked as they laid out a stretcher for Loni.

"We were dancing, and she couldn't catch her breath," Manny spoke up, and Kit was surprised, she'd almost forgotten he was there. "Then, suddenly, she started gasping like she was choking on air. I patted her back, and it seemed like it helped; she coughed, but it was so bad that she passed out."

"Ruthie said she fell last night, said it looked like she fainted," Carly walked over with the tiny blonde girl behind her, looking teary-eyed and scared. "Loni made her promise not to tell you."

"What? Why?" Luca questioned. "Why would she not tell us that!?"

"I'm sorry," Ruthie cried as tears ran down her little face.

"It's okay Ruthie, thanks for telling us," Kit's dad Stone spoke to her, always coming in the clutch. "Luca and Kit aren't mad at ya, okay? They're just worried bout Loni."

Kit's heart ached, but she simply nodded. Loni was all she could focus on, and Luca too. Carly got it and quickly scooped Ruthie up, walking away as she whispered soothing words.

"She was struggling to breathe when we got to her; she responded to CPR but seems to have a lot of fluid in her lungs," Kit told the paramedics in a shaky voice; she was losing her grip quickly, and Luca just looked lost. When it came to his daughters, especially Loni, because she was sensitive, he was so protective. This was something he couldn't shield her from and it had to be killing him.

They lifted Loni onto the stretcher and started taking her vitals. As they rolled her, our Luca and Kit were right behind them, and she could hear everyone else following too.

"Her pulse is low. Let's get her on oxygen."

"Has she been sick?"

"No." Kit said, "but she said her stomach felt funny today like she was nervous."

They wheeled the stretcher into the van, and Luca climbed in beside her. When they strapped the oxygen to her mouth, Loni's brown eyes widened in fear, and Luca took her hand, calming her with soft words.

She looked so tiny, lying there strapped to a stretcher with oxygen over her little face.

Sixteen years was nothing, nothing at all, Loni was just a baby, and she'd never looked smaller then at that moment.

Loni passed out in the ambulance on the way to the hospital; thankfully, her pulse remained steady, with the oxygen she was on.

A large group of doctors lead them inside the urgency room, as the paramedics wheeled Loni in. They raced inside so fast that Kit nearly tripped had Luca not held tightly to her arm.

"Wait here." A nurse stopped them from going further as several doctors followed the paramedics into a room with Loni.

"Where are you taking her? What's happening!" Luca pushed forward, but a few other doctors stopped him.

"You have to let them help her." One of them was saying.

"Kit, Luca!" Kit turned to see a large group rushing towards them, led by Carly and Andre.

"We came right behind you; where is she?" Andre asked.

Kit motioned to the room they'd taken Loni. She was starting to go numb, any strength she'd pulled out earlier, was depleting fast. Luca seemed to sense it. He put his arm around her, pulling her into his side.

The door they'd just sent Loni through opened suddenly, and she was being pushed along on a gurney.

"Where are you going? What's happening?" Luca demanded as he raced after them.

A doctor, an older man with black hair streaked with grey, in dark blue scrubs, stopped and looked at him.

"I'm Dr. Gupta, head of the emergency. Right now, we need to focus on your daughter. We're bringing her up to cardiology. We need you to please stay here and out of the way. I will be back to talk to you with the head of cardiology as soon as we can."

He spun around then and they were gone faster than Kit could fully comprehend his words.

"Cardiology," Luca gulped, and he and Andre exchanged glances.

"Our mom," Andre stifled a sob.

Their mom had died from complications from a heart condition when they were little boys... was that.. oh god! Kit's eyes widened as her heart filled with dread.

"She inherited it, the heart condition?" Kit guessed as her world felt like it was crashing down.

"We don't know anything yet, don't get ahead of yourselves," Carly said.

"We know she stopped breathing and passed out! We know they're taking to her the head of cardiology, the head!" Luca cried out.

A small whimper caught her and Luca's attention, and Kit's gaze quickly found Lissa. She was wearing Stone's flannel, and it swallowed her small frame. Her little spitfire looked so tiny and scared.

"Shit, Lissa, I didn't mean"- Luca winced.

"Come here, baby," Kit said, and Lissa ran to her and Luca, burying her face in Luca's chest as he pulled her close.

Luca whispered soothing words to her as Kit stroked her hair.

"My mom will be here soon to pick up Len and Ruthie. I can ask her to take Lissa too." Carly offered.

"No!" Lissa looked at Kit with teary blue eyes. "I can't leave my sister, please, mom."

"I'll be good," she added with a quivering lip.

"We know you will," Luca gave Kit a look, and she nodded.

In a similar situation there was no way would Luca leave his brother. Kit felt similar about the cousin she grew up with, and had she ever known her siblings, she'd not have left them either.

"She can stay," Kit said, stroking Lissa's hair.

"She's here, Carly," Andre had each twin by the hand, and Carly nodded and headed toward him.

"I'll be right back," Carly promised; she glanced at Kit and then down at Lissa. "Lissa, do you want to walk with us outside? Get out of here for a little bit, at least?"

The little girl sniffled but took Carly's hand and walked with her.

Kit was grateful because she knew Carly would tell Lissa what she wanted to hear. Kit couldn't bring herself to make promises when she was so unsure and scared.

She felt a cold shock tonight like nothing she'd ever felt, and it was still there. Something was very, very wrong with Loni.

Kit finally took in the rest of the waiting room. Andrea and her mom were sitting along with a few other girls. Next to them sat Manny, who was looking down at his lap.

Stone caught Kit's eye and walked over toward them. He rested a hand on Luca's shoulder and then hugged Kit.

"Loni's a tough girl," Stone offered. "Don't forget that. She'll get through this."

"She has to," Kit whispered. "I can't lose her. I can't lose my baby girl."

"You won't, we won't," Luca pulled her into his arms. "I don't care what I have to do. We aren't losing her, Cricket. Do you hear me? We aren't."

She couldn't hold it in anymore and started breaking down, soaking her husband's chest with tears as he held her tightly.

"We aren't losing her." He repeated over and over.

If only she believed him.

After a sixteen-hour shift, Gus Blake was more than ready to slip out of bright white hospital lights and into the soft yellow hue of a bar.

He didn't drink often, but it had been a long week. It started great, the young doctor had been proving himself. He was even given a special case, he'd found a rare diagnosis, treated it, and it went well. His higher ups were impressed, for once he was making a name for himself outside of the huge shadow that followed him.

He should've been floating on air. Unfortunately, it swallowed up all his time, all week. She wasn't happy. Not at all.

Being a doctor would always be this way. What was he going to do if she never understood?

He knew that he should be going home to her and making things right. She'd been the one light in his life after so many dark days.

But after that fight this morning, he needed some beers and at least one ear to hear his side.

As Gus headed towards the community locker room to change, a bunch of commotion stopped him.

Several doctors was rushing by with a girl on a gurney. Something unexplainable pulled at him. He ran to catch up with them. They were racing her to the cardiology department.

"What's going on?" He asked one of his colleagues.

"Sixteen-year-old girl, presenting with heart failure."

"What!? Heart failure at sixteen?"

Doctor Gupta heard his voice and whirled around.

"Dr. Blake. Call your dad."

"But .. he's retired"-

A flash of understanding passed over the older doctors face, as he sighed.

"I know he is and I know why, but he's the best damn cardiologist in the state. We need him on this."

Gus gulped and nodded. "I'll call him."

The group of doctors wheeled the girl into the room. Gus watched the door shut as he pulled his cell phone out.

His long week, desire for drinks, relationship woes, and everything else was long forgotten.

Chapter 5

As they all sat and waited, the time seemed to tick by. The waiting room was so silent. Aside from an occasional sniffle from someone stifling back tears, you could hear a pin drop.

Sitting there like that reminded Luca Donato of the worst day of his life. In that same hospital nearly seventeen years ago, Kit, Andre, and Carly sat and waited to say goodbye to his dad, Leonardo. It was there in that hospital they watched him take his last breath.

Ultimately it led to the best day, as that was also the night Loni was conceived. He and Kit hadn't been careful in their grief as they sought comfort in each other, but they both knew she was a gift. Leondra was a gift from his dad, and so they named her after him.

As Luca sat there, he realized that wasn't the worst day; it wasn't even close. There wasn't even a word to describe the feeling of seeing his daughter passed out and unable to breathe. Terrified and helpless were probably the closest, but even those didn't feel strong enough.

He wanted to scream, punch a wall, get wasted, something, anything, to not feel like this.

But....he couldn't do any of those things.

All he could do was sit there, holding his wife's hand, stroking his other daughters hair, while they waited endlessly for news.

Eventually, two girls sitting next to Loni's long-time friend, Andrea, got up to leave. Andrea stayed but promised she'd call them with any news.

The elevator doors opened, the doctor from earlier stepped out, and everyone started talking at once.

"Is she okay?"

"Where's Loni?"

"Can we see her?"

"She's stable; not awake yet," the doctor said. "Let's get some of you moved up to cardiology. Visiting hours are over, but I told the nurses to be lenient tonight. I do have to ask for everyone but family to leave though, I'm sorry."

The group started to stand, everyone stiff from having sat for so long.

Andrea's mom, Cathy, glanced towards Kit, "Kit, call me if you need anything. We will be back tomorrow morning."

"Thanks, Cathy," Kit said softly as she and Andrea left.

"Can you call me if anything changes?" Manny asked, "I can be right back here."

"Yeah, of course, " Luca agreed.

"I'll clean up the restaurant, so you don't need to worry about it."

"You don't have to do that," Kit protested.

"I need to do something," Manny replied.

"You're a good kid, Manny. Thanks," Luca offered.

Manny nodded and followed Andrea and her mom out. To think, earlier today, Luca's biggest problem was accepting Loni's desire to date Manny. He'd give anything for that to be his only worry right now. Hell he'd even drive them to Vegas if it meant Loni would be okay.

The rest of the family walked unto the elevator to head up to cardiology. Luca followed them all on; everyone was quiet, even Lissa. The mood was heavy as the elevator rose to the top floor.

It was a large and quiet wing that, Dr. Gupta, according to his name tag, brought them to. There was a waiting area in the center with a few couches and chairs near a large desk where a few nurses sat. Behind them were two large doors that said cardiology staff only.

There were several closed-door rooms; Luca immediately noticed that one said Leondra Ann Donato on it.

Dr. Gupta motioned for Kit and Luca to follow him to the room next to hers. It was a small room with the name Georgina Morgan MD, Head of Cardiology, on it.

Dr. Morgan looked up from the files and stuff on her desk as they stepped in, she was wearing an official looking white coat with her name tag on it. Her black hair was cut short and left naturally curly, while a pair of glasses rested on her nose. Dr. Gupta walked in and stood behind her, holding some files in his arms. His face was a bit more weathered then hers and his hair was streaked with gray.

"Come sit down, Mr. and Mrs. Donato," she said. "I'm Dr. Morgan, and this is Dr. Gupta."

"Kit and Luca," Kit offered quietly. "How is Loni?"

"is she okay? What's going on?" Luca added as he reluctantly sat down with Kit.

"First of all, we did stabilize her. She's currently resting, but she'll likely wake up for a bit tonight, and you can talk to her."

"What happened? Why did she stop breathing?" Kit asked.

"There's not an easy way to say this. Your daughter is in heart failure."

Kit gasped, and Luca's own heart felt like it dropped into his stomach right there and then.

"Heart failure?" He managed to croak out.

"I know how scary that sounds, and it is. However, we have treated much older patients with heart failure successfully. What I suspect, and I'm waiting for the results of a few more tests first, but I looked into the family history; and I believe Loni has the same heart condition your mother had."

"No," Kit whimpered, and Luca took her hand.

"They tested her for it, both girls, when they were babies," Luca protested as if that could somehow make this not be true.

"It's called the brugada syndrome, and it can often lay dormant, undetected for years. There isn't a way they would have caught it when she was a baby. It only shows up in tests if symptoms are present. Its rare, the condition, and so is inheriting it, so they probably didn't think you needed continuous tests."

"I didn't even know it had a name," Luca mumbled. "So it's why she stopped breathing?"

"Yes. Burgada most commonly causes dizziness, seizures, gasping, and difficulty catching your breath. The more dangerous symptoms are fainting and rapid and irregular heart rate, sometimes even extremely rapid, which can be very concerning. Left untreated, it can lead to cardiac arrest, even sudden death."

"Oh god," Kit gasped as a chill descended Luca's spine.

"But it is treatable?" Luca questioned. "Times have changed since my mom...right? There are things you can do?"

"It is treatable. However, the most common treatment is a implantable cardioverter defibrillator. This is a device we'd implant into Loni's chest that would regulate her heart."

"So do it."

"I wish we could. The problem is that Loni's heart is severely inflamed and damaged. I believe her condition started to present itself at least a month ago. She probably didn't notice it or just thought she felt anxious. I also believe she may have had a mild heart attack recently."

"What!?" Luca and Kit both cried at the same time.

"Likely in her sleep, and she didn't even realize it," Dr. Morgan said gently. "This is why I highly reccomend your other daughter be tested soon and continue to get tested yearly. Early detection would have prevented this."

"Of course, we will..." Kit stammered. "Loni never- I guess she did talk about getting head rushes from painting a few times. She gets so zoned in, I didn't think it was anything more then her eyes needing a break. A heart attack? How did I miss this?"

"She's been working with me at Leo's, was it all to much? Why didn't I see it?" Luca added, they'd been spending so much time together lately. How did he miss this?

"Don't be hard on yourselves," Dr. Gupta assured them. "These symptoms are not obvious."

"He's right. There is a reason why heart disease is called a silent killer. Often things have already progressed by the time we even see any symptoms," Dr. Morgan added.

"What do we do now?" Luca asked.

"I was able to drain the fluid from her lungs. I have her on a strong inflammatory and a beta blocker. I hope it'll get her out of heart failure, so we can then determine the next steps to treat her heart condition."

"You hope? So you don't know?" Luca cried out.

"Unfortunately, right now, it is a wait-and-see. Beta-blockers are usually successful in treating health failure, but sometimes it can get worse before it gets better. So don't be alarmed if she's frail, exhausted, and showing other symptoms over the next few days."

"Will she stop breathing again?" Kit asked in a trembling voice.

"We have her on machines that'll keep her breathing, and we're monitoring her twenty-four seven. We have a call out to one of the best cardiologists in the country. We lucked out in that his son works here and called him tonight. Jonathan

Blake, he's out of the country now but said he'll be here by the end of the week."

Having one of the best cardiologists on her case should have made Luca feel better, but instead, it only reinforced how bad this was.

"I know how dire this all is," Dr. Morgan leaned in, her brown eyes full of warmth, despite the awful news she'd had to share with them. "Just know that no one here is giving up hope. Positivity will go a long way here, okay?"

Luca gulped, and Kit sniffled back a few years.

"Can we go sit with her now?" Luca asked as he stood and pulled Kit up with him.

"I want to check on her again, and then yes. She'll hopefully wake up soon. I'll come out and get you when you can see her."

They left the office and headed back to the waiting room, where everyone looked up for answers.

"She's stable, for now," Luca said. "She should be awake soon."

"What"- Stone started to speak.

"Heart failure," Kit cut him off as her lip trembled.

"What!?" Carly gasped.

"Oh no," Andre breathed out as he stood and took a step towards them.

"What does that mean, mom?" Lissa asked. "Is Loni gonna be okay?"

"Lissa." Kit looked at her and then the clock, "Oh God, did you even eat dinner?"

"I didn't think about it, mom. It's okay," Lissa replied.

"There's a little cafeteria right around the corner," a nurse offered as she walked by. "There are vending machines with various stuff. Even a decent sandwich machine."

"Honey, why don't you get a bunch of snacks for everyone while talk to your grandpa, uncle and aunt?" Kit suggested as she handed Lissa some bills from her purse.

"Okay, I'll be right back." Lissa took it and dashed off around the corner.

"I forgot to feed her. I'm a terrible mother," Kit cried out as she fell to her knees.

"No. No, you're not I, didn't remember to either, and she didn't even think about it. We're all distracted." Luca knelt beside Kit and pulled her into his arms.

"Kit listen to him, you're a wonderful mother," Carly added.

"Then how did I not see it? How did I not sense it? They said she's probably been showing symptoms for a month! They said she may have had a heart attack!" Kit cried out as tears ran down her face.

"She said she probably thought it was nothing," Luca reminded her. "Like at breakfast when she said her belly felt funny. We assumed it was nerves."

"It was her heart... my god. My poor baby's heart," Kit sobbed as Luca held her close.

Gus was finally getting changed and ready to head out when his cell rang and of course, it was her.

He sighed as he picked up the call, "I know you're mad, but"-

"Where are you?" She demanded.

"I'm leaving here soon. Something came up."-

"Something always comes up!" She cut him off, "you're at the bar, right?"

"That's where I was headed," he admitted. "Come meet me, and let's talk."

"You want to talk in public? Why? Are you breaking up with me?"

"No, Jenny," he sighed. Sometimes she made him want to bang his head against the nearest wall. "It's been a long day, starting, with our fight this morning."

Ending with having to call his dad and ask for help with a case. Not just any case, a teenage girl, this wouldn't be easy, on either of them.

"The fight was your fault! You promised you'd be at that party."

"I tried!" As he yelled, a few changing doctors looked over at him.

Embarrassed, he ducked out of the locker room.

"I told you I had a special case, Jenny," he said in a lower voice as he ducked down the corridor. "I can't control that he had a flare-up the day of the party, but I have to put my patients first."

"I'm trying to understand that. I am! But when do I get to be first? Ever?"

"I'm trying. I'm a new doctor; I have to prove myself."

"Life balance matters, Gus," she pointed out. "As a doctor, you should know that."

This is why so many of his colleagues remained single. He stepped into the cafeteria and stopped short as his eyes took in a little red-headed girl, a coppery shade just like hers. Her back was to him, and she hadn't seen him yet. It was silly, just a hair color, yet it was enough to bring all those childhood memories to the fringes of his head.

"Gus? Are you still there?"

"You stupid piece of the crap machine!" The girl suddenly did some crazy spin kick to the machine, effectively pulling Gus from his stupor and making him laugh at the same time.

"Gus! What's going on?"

"I got to go; I'll be home soon, okay?"

"I thought you wanted to meet at the bar?"

"I'll call you." He hung up, knowing he had just made it worse.

"What did the vending machine ever do to you?" he asked as he approached the girl.

She whirled around, and he saw her face was much older than he pegged her for. He'd assumed eight to ten based on her small stature, but she looked to be about twelve or thirteen.

"It's not working!" She shouted irritably. "This is what Loni usually does! She takes care of everyone but she's super sick and she can't, so I have to, and I suck at it!"

"Loni... that's the girl they brought in tonight," Gus softened his voice and stuck a few bills in the machine. "She your sister?"

"Yeah. I'm Lissa."

"Dr. Blake," he selected the number for the stuck sandwich, forcing the stuck one and a new one to fall.

"I need like four more of those," Lissa said, and Gus went ahead and bought them for her.

"Thanks," she said as he handed them to her.

"You're here for your sister. You're staying out of everyone's way; that's all anyone can ask of you."

"If it were me in there, Loni would be caring for everyone. I know she would."

"Maybe, but you don't have to be her, okay? No one is expecting you to."

"I never saw my parents so upset," Lissa said quietly. "I know this is bad."

Her tears spilled over, and Gus took her arm, leading her to a chair. She set the sandwiches down in the empty one next to her.

"I'm not going to lie to you. I get the feeling you don't like that."

"No. I don't," she agreed.

"You're right. What's going on with your sister is very serious. But - everyone here is rooting for her. Everyone."

"Will they be able to help her?"

"We are going to everything we can. My dad is even coming and is one of the best doctors ever. She's in great hands here."

"I sure hope so," Lissa sighed as she wiped her eyes dry. "I have been trying so hard not to cry. I don't want my mom and dad to worry about me too."

"It's okay to be scared and upset," he offered. "If you need to get away from everyone for a moment. Right behind those pop machines, there is a little hallway. It leads to an old lab no one uses anymore. It's a good spot to cry."

"Thanks," she took a breath as she calmed herself. "You're nice, Dr. Blake."

"I've been exactly where you are."

She looked up at him for clarification.

"Trying to care for my parents on the worst night of their lives." A shudder went through his body; why did tonight remind him so much of that night?

"Lissa?" A woman called, and Lissa looked past Gus towards the voice as her footsteps grew closer.

"Sorry, mom. The machine got stuck, and this doctor helped me."

Gus turned around to greet the woman and nearly dropped to the ground. "You... you look just like her," he stuttered out.

Same coppery red hair, same honey-brown eyes, and even how she tilted her head in confusion, it was all so similar...

How was this possible?

"Like who? Do I know you?" The woman asked as Lissa gathered her sandwiches and joined her.

"Kit, she's awake!" A male voice yelled out.

"Oh, thank god! We got to go!"

The woman, Kit, took Lissa's hand, and they rushed off, leaving Gus standing there stunned and confused.

Chapter 6

"And I'll be wearing white when I come into your kingdom. I'm as green as the ring on my little cold finger."

On year ten, the mother sat patiently on top of a blanket in the center of the field of flowers. She'd packed a picnic lunch and even indulged in cupcakes with pink frosting.

Finally, a familiar dark blue car pulled up, stopping at the field's edge. London jumped out in her pretty flowery dress, all smiles as she waved happily.

Waving back at her daughter, her smile faded when the car pulled away.

She'd hoped he would come today too...

She pushed her self-pity aside as she stood and held her arms out for her beautiful ten-year-old girl.

"Hi!" London raced into her arms, smelling like a field of strawberries with a hint of vanilla. If only she could bottle up that scent.

"Happy birthday, London." She kissed the top of her head.

"Thanks, mom!"

She sometimes mourned for the days when her children called her mama and mommy. Mom was just more proof they were growing up.

"How was your night at your dad's?"

"Good. His apartment is tiny, though," London said as she flipped her long and messy braid over her shoulder.

She had likely done that herself. Her father could perform literal medical miracles on people, but a braid? Not so much.

"Your brother didn't want to spend the day with us?"

"No, dad's going to let him do his rounds with him."

"Today? But it's your birthday," the mother frowned.

"We had a little party last night and a birthday breakfast; it's okay!"

Unfazed, London moved on toward the rose bushes, which were finally back in bloom after a few years of being dormant.

"The roses are back this year! They are so pretty!" London plopped down with what looked like a new sketchbook and some colored pencils.

"Did you get that for your birthday?"

"Yeah, from Nancy."

"Who is Nancy?"

"Dad's new friend, she lives next door. She made my cake for my party last night!" London smiled, blissfully unaware that her mother's gut twisted with that news.

Still, she kept an even-tempered smile on her face. "How nice of her."

Moving on, already? The ink was barely even dry. Could she really blame him, though? It was all her fault. Of course, he left, and her son chose to go with him. Everyone, even her sweet London, would leave her someday. It was the poetic justice she deserved.

"Well, I guess it's just us girls today," she tucked an arm around her daughter, and London rested her head on her shoulder. "What should we do?"

"Can we stay here for a while? It's my favorite place in the whole world." London declared that every time they came here, it always made the mother smile.

"Mine too," she cuddled her little girl close. "Promise me something?"

"What?" London asked.

"Promise me that no matter what happens, we'll always come back here on this special day, just the two of us."

"I promise."

Loni was confused and dizzy when she opened her eyes; the room was so blindingly white it took her a moment to focus.

A dark-haired woman in a white coat stood beside her, "it's okay, Loni." Her voice was calm and soothing. "You're in the hospital. Your parents will be"-

"Loni!" Luca was at her bedside in the next instant.

"Right in," the doctor finished with a soft chuckle.

"Dad? Where's?"

"Loni, oh thank god you're awake," Kit answered her question as she ran into the room with Lissa right behind her.

Kit was rushing to the other side of Loni, resting her hand on her shoulder.

"Wh.. what happened?" Loni tried to sit up, but her chest felt so heavy it was like she was chained to the bed. She realized then there were weird tubes and stuff all over her. Something under her nose blew air up her nostrils; it felt so funny.

"Loni, I'm Dr. Morgan," The doctor spoke up, as she used a remote to raise the bed so Loni could see better. "I know it's scary to wake up in the hospital. But you're in good hands here, okay?"

"Okay," Loni frowned; she had a bad feeling. "The last thing I remember is dancing with Manny."

"Your heart rate got too high, and it caused you to stop breathing and lose consciousness. There are some things going on with your heart, but we'll talk more in detail about it tomorrow. For tonight, I want you resting."

"I think that's a good idea," Luca agreed.

"She hadn't had dinner. I don't think she's eaten a thing today," Kit said, her face full of concern as it washed over Loni's face.

"I don't feel hungry," Loni said; food was the last thing on her mind. She was mainly confused, her body felt weird, kind of like after a long run, when you just wanted to collapse. She also felt so weak and tired.

"We have her on an IV, no solid food for right now," the doctor said. "Loni, I'm going to leave you to chat with your parents, but I'll be in to check on you again before lights out."

"Okay, Dr. Morgan."

Dr. Morgan directed her attention to Kit and Luca. "The visiting hours are over at nine. You three can stay. The others will need to leave, but if they want to pop in and see Loni before they leave, that's fine."

"Okay, I'll grab them in a moment," Kit agreed.

"Lights are out at ten and if you're staying here we ask not to be out and about too much after that time. As long as Loni is in critical condition, we let the parents stay overnights here. I'll be setting up an on-call room for you. For tonight you three can stay in here. I'll have a nurse bring a few beds in."

Critical condition? Loni felt a chill go down her spine at those words.

"Thank you," Luca said, "we wouldn't have left, so I'm glad you're letting us stay."

"I know," Dr. Morgan smiled lightly. "But you do need to take care of yourselves. I do not want you two here twenty.-four-seven. I'll lecture you more about that tomorrow, though."

"What about Lissa? I know she can stay tonight- but?" Kit asked.

"I'll make an exception and it's up to you two, but she shouldn't be here every night," Dr. Morgan said and her mom nodded. "We'll talk more tomorrow, and set up those tests we talked about too."

"Thank you," Kit agreed.

Dr. Morgan left the room, and Loni looked at Kit first, whose eyes were all puffy and red.

"Mom, you look awful. Don't cry anymore, okay? I'll be alright." She didn't know if that was true, but she had such a strong urge to make her mom to feel better.

"You scared us so much, baby," Kit stroked her cheek.

"I'm sorry," Loni whispered.

"Oh sweet Loni, it's okay, you just got to be strong and get better for us."

"I will, mom."

"How are you feeling?" Luca asked, and she turned to look at him. He looked so tired and his eyes were puffy too.

"I'm just exhausted mostly."

"You have to be honest with the doctors and us. Even if something seems minor, you need to tell us, Loni."

"I will," she gulped. "I passed out last night."

"We know, Ruthie told us."

"Oh gosh, she must feel awful!"

"She'll be okay," Kit said in an assuring tone.

Loni spied Lissa then in the corner, so quiet and pale, and quiet and Lissa did not usually go hand in hand.

"Lissa, come over here," Loni urged her little sister, and she took a few steps forward, sitting gingerly on the edge of the bed.

"You okay?"

"I was so scared, Loni. I thought.. " Tears started to spill down Lissa's cheeks. "You can't die, okay? Please! Don't die!"

Loni felt tears burn his eyes as a lump formed in her throat. "I'm not - oh Lissa."

Her little sister broke into sobs then and Loni bet she'd been holding it in all night.

"Shorty, come here," Luca was up in moments, wrapping her little sister in a big hug. "It's okay, baby. I know it was a scary day. I'm here, okay, let it all out."

He whispered soothing words to Lissa as her sobs slowly subsided.

Kit started crying, and Loni quickly took her hand, holding it to her cheek.

"It's okay, mom, everything will be okay," Loni promised again.

"Lissa, you hear me too, " Loni demanded. "I'm not going to die."

"You better not!" Lissa sniffled. "I need my big sister."

"Oh Lissa," Kit choked out. We all need her."

"I will be fine," Loni assured them again, but somehow Lissa saying she could die made that knot in her stomach so much bigger.

"You have to be who else am I going to annoy everyday?" Lissa said as she wiped a hand over her wet face.

"I'm not going to die. I can't. That would leave you in charge of Leo's."

"That would be a disaster," Luca joked, "everyone dancing on tables, she'd probably bedazzle the entire bar."

"It would make it pretty!" Lissa giggled through her tears, she looked to be calming down.

Kit was stroking Loni's hair softly, she'd also stopped crying, but Loni could see she was on the verge of it again. Her dad moved from Lissa over to Kit, sitting on the edge of the bed with her and placing a hand on her shoulder.

"Hey...can we come in?" Carly stepped in and Andre and her grandpa were behind her.

"Of course," Loni agreed.

"I know we can't stay long, but we wanted to stay goodnight," Andre offered her a soft smile. "How are you feeling?"

"Kind of weird, really tired," Loni offered.

"Some birthday, huh?" Stone stepped over to her bedside and ruffled her hair. "Soon as you leave, I'll take you anywhere you want. We can even go get you your first tattoo."

"Dad, she's sixteen, not eighteen," Kit scolded as Luca laughed.

"Sixteen, with permission, I looked it up!"

"She's not getting a tattoo!" Kit protested.

"A rose might be pretty, though," Loni mused. "I could design it myself."

"Luca. Tell her no."

"I mean...if it was small, maybe.."

"Luca!" She whispered harshly.

"Why not?" Luca asked, surprising her; she never knew what he'd be cool with. "I have a few, and you have one."

"You do?" Loni and Lissa both asked Kit once.

Carly giggled, "oops."

"What is it?" Loni asked excitedly.

"Where is it?" Lissa asked, "we've never seen it."

"Look what you did, " Kit said to Luca.

"Is it dads name?" Loni guessed. "I bet it is."

Her dad had her mom's full name, Cricket, tattooed into a heart on his chest. Later he added both Leondra and then Elisabeth under it in creative-looking banners.

"I bet so too!" Lissa agreed.

"It is," Kit confirmed. "It's the words Ti Amo, Luciano, Sempre. Which means I love you, Luciano, always."

"That's so sweet," Loni sighed dreamily as her parents locked gazes.

"Is it on your boob?" Lissa asked bluntly.

Carly and Andre laughed, and Stone cringed.

"I'll show you someday," Kit said in an amused tone. "And no tattoos for you two until you're eighteen.'"

"Your dad and I will talk her into it." Stone winked at Loni and then kissed her forehead.

"You're both lucky I'm too drained to kill you," Kit muttered.

"Oh my gosh, Lucky! He's been alone all night!" Loni suddenly realized, filling with panic. "He's probably so worried."

"He's fine," Carly assured her. "Ruthie said she's been taking good care of him for you."

"We got him until you're out," Andre added. "Don't you worry about anything but getting better, Loni."

"Thanks, uncle Andre."

Poor Lucky! he was a family dog, but he and Loni had a special bond. He slept with Loni every night since they had him. He was probably so upset without her. She just hoped he could sleep.

"We should get going; the nurses keep walking by and looking in." Carly stepped over and squeezed her hand. "We'll be back to see you tomorrow; you sleep well and heal up, okay?"

"I will," Loni promised.

"We love you, " Andre added as he patted his hand.

"Love you guys too; I'll be fine, don't worry." Loni once again felt an urge to assure despite feeling so totally unsure.

"I'll walk you out," Kit offered. "I need to use the restroom anyway."

"Me too," Lissa got off the bed to follow.

As everyone left, the room fell silent, and Luca sat on the edge of her bed. "You don't have to keep up all that tough stuff. How are you really doing?"

"I'm scared," she admitted and it did feel good to say it out loud.

A storm of emotions passed through his eyes. "I am too."

"Daddy," she whimpered.

He put an arm around her and she nestled her head into the crook of his arm, just like she used to do when she was little.

"It's okay to be scared. It's also okay to feel angry or sad or whatever you feel, whenever you feel it. You don't have to pretend for me, or mom either. Okay?"

"Okay," she sniffled.

"I am scared as hell. But I won't for one second lose hope. I will fight to the ends of the earth for you, pumpkin. We will get through this."

His words felt soothing and that terrible uneasy pit in her stomach eased up some. She curled up closer, and he stroked her hair.

"No matter what, Loni, you got to keep fighting. You can't give up hope. Will you promise me that?"

"I promise."

Chapter 7

"What happened to you? You look terrible," Dr. Gupta said bluntly as Gus drug his tired self into the hospital.

"Fought with Jenny," he explained, although that was only the tip of it. He'd had nightmares about that night, and it kept him up all night.

Dr. Gupta let out a little tsk sound but offered no advice. He'd been a great mentor to Gus but was never a fan of Jenny. Dr. Gupta felt she needed to be more supportive, and maybe he was right, but Gus wasn't there for her enough, either. They were at crossroads in their relationship, and he didn't know what to do. It didn't help that he didn't even have time to sit and think about it, either.

"Well, clear your head. It needs to be fresh. We're adding you to the Donato case."

Gus nodded; he expected as much. After all the effort to get out from under his dad's shadow, this would put him right back in it. The experience would be priceless, though, and he knew that.

"Head on up to cardiology. Dr. Morgan is checking in with Loni and her parents now, but her team is meeting in her room next door."

"Okay, I'll head right up. Thanks, Dr. Gupta."

He hurried to cardiology and found Lissa talking to a teenage boy in the waiting room. He had a box of donuts next to him on the table. Along with a gift bag, a box of chocolates, and some flowers.

"Hi, Dr. Blake," Lissa greeted him. She was still in the same clothes, so they'd likely spent the night.

"Hey, Lissa. Ninja kick any vending machines this morning?" Gus asked, and she shook her head and giggled.

"Nope, didn't have to; Manny brought donuts!"

"I see that," Gus noted.

"Is it okay that I brought Loni this stuff?" Manny asked Gus.

"She can't have the chocolates yet, but everything else, sure! It's nice to brighten up those boring rooms."

"Okay, thanks," Manny said as he ran a hand through his hair. "I hope I can see her today. The other doctor said it depends on how she feels after they talk."

"If you want, I can take your number and text you when she can see people," Gus offered.

"No, it's okay. I'd rather just wait here." His eyes darted toward her room for a moment.

"Hiya Shorty!" A booming voice called from behind.

"Grandpa!" Lissa cheered as she bounced off her chair.

Gus turned to see an older guy in a backward hat and a loose flannel walking up. He must be the mom's dad, as Gus recalled the doctors talking about how the dad's dad had died years earlier in this hospital. He scooped Lissa up and hugged her before setting her back down.

"This is Dr. Blake," Lissa introduced the two. "This is my grandpa, Stone."

"How is Loni this morning?" Stone asked.

"I'm just getting in, but I'll let you know as soon as there's an update," Gus offered.

"Do I know you?" Stone asked.

"I don't think so," Gus said, taking a step back from the strong scent coming off him.

"You look really familiar... ever come into Willow Grill?" Stone tilted his head and studied him.

"No, I frequent the bar closest to the hospital."

"Must just be one of those faces, then," Stone shrugged it off and sat next to Manny. "Here already? Good kid."

"Yeah, don't think I slept a wink."

Gus left them to chat and ducked into Dr. Morgan's office. The rest of the team was already sitting and talking. He sat and started sorting through a stack of old case files with the name Elizabeth Donato.

"Loni's grandmother on the dad's side," Dr. Banz said as he noted what Gus was looking at. "Same heart condition. Although it's presenting more severe in Loni's case."

"Interesting," Gus mumbled as he sorted through the files. "Strong woman; she had two sons while living with this."

"Amazing, actually," someone else said.

"The grandpa had lung cancer," another doctor mentioned. "Later in life, though. Doesn't seem to be connected."

She passed the file over to Gus to look at.

"What about the mom's history? I just met the grandpa from Loni's mom's side, and he seems healthy, although he reeked like a weed," Gus noted.

"Go, gramps," an intern snickered, and Gus just rolled his eyes

"We should pull the mom's full medical history too. I know Elizabeth's case will be the most important thing to look at. But I want to ensure we're not missing anything else in the family history." Gus knew that would be one of his dad's first requests.

"On it." Another intern said as she hustled out of the room.

He still couldn't get quite over how similar Loni's mom looked to...her.

Was there a connection here? It couldn't be, it wasn't possible, but it sure was strange.

Gus couldn't shake the weird feeling and was anxious to see those records.

"What do you mean my heart is failing?" A panicked Loni asked.

Dr. Morgan had spent a good bit of time explaining what happened and what was going on with Loni now, as Luca and Kit sat at her bedside.

Loni could wrap her head around inheriting her grandma Elizabeth's heart condition. The symptoms all made sense, and she realized her head rushes, heart racing, and weird flutters were all suddenly not, the nothing, she'd kept telling herself they were.

However, a heart attack in her sleep? Heart failure!? These aren't things that happen to teenagers? How could this all be true?

Suddenly Lissa's teary face from last night was in her head. "Don't die!" She could... this was that serious.

Her heart started to accelerate as the panic increased and the doctor's eyes filled with worry.

"It's okay; stay calm, Loni, " Dr. Morgan said softly. "I want you to take a deep breath in and out, okay? In and out."

Luca squeezed her hand as she breathed, the oxygen under her nose assisting her. Slowly but surely, her heart rate returned to normal.

"Is that from the condition too? When I get nervous and my heart pounds?"

"Nerves and anxiety are normal. Your heart increasing to scary news and things like that is also normal." Dr. Morgan explained. "The hard part about Brugada can be determining when your heart is reacting normally to a situation or when you have a flare up. Sometimes, both can occur at the same time."

She paused to let that set in before continuing. "Some of the machines you're hooked up to are helping your heart to keep beating, but they can't stop it from beating too fast. You just press this button here if you start feeling your heart race, okay?"

"Okay," Loni gulped nervously.

"The monitors will also alert us to any changes. I'm right next door and have an entire team on your case," Dr. Morgan assured her. "We're going to do everything we can for you."

"And the drugs I'm on might worsen me before I get better? How much worse?"

"We really won't know until the symptoms start to show," she confirmed.

"So I'm going to be here for a while," Loni guessed.

"Make yourself at home," Dr. Morgan said gently.

"You okay, honey?" Kit asked, "I know that was a lot to take in."

"Yeah..." she started, then looked at her dad's knowing face. "Honestly, no, I'm scared, and it's a lot."

"I know it is," Kit agreed with a sigh.

"It's okay to be scared, but try and stay positive. Stress won't help your situation." The doctor looked up at the clock and then back at her parents. "Have you two been home yet?"

"No," Luca said. "And we're not leaving."

"You need to take care of yourselves, too," Dr. Morgan advised. "I've booked an on-call room for you. It's just two doors from my office. However, please go home for at least a few hours each day. You need rest, food, and showers. I've seen far too many parents end up hospitalized themselves. Loni needs your strength."

"What if we take turns going home?" Kit asked Luca. "I can take Lissa with me."

"That'll work," Luca agreed. "I'm sure Carly and Andre will be here soon."

"Since Loni feels fairly good right now, she can have visitors. No more than two at a time, though," Dr. Morgan said, "maybe the three of you should all go home and regroup while we let a visitors or two in the waiting room spend some time with Loni."

"I don't know..." Luca hesitated.

"If anything happens, I will call you immediately. You two should talk to Lissa about all this outside of the hospital. I set up a time at two today to test her for Brugada. The idea could freak her out."

"Freaks me out," Luca muttered.

"Lissa could have this too?" Loni asked worriedly.

"It's very rare so likely not, but we'd rather be safe," Dr. Morgan said.

"I hope you're right," Kit sighed. "Are you sure you're okay here, Loni? We won't be gone long."

"Go, please," Loni urged them. "I'll be fine here until you get back."

"Call us if anything changes," Luca said firmly. "We'll be back here in five minutes if need be."

"I will," Dr. Morgan promised him.

Kit ran a hand through Loni's hair. "What can I bring back for you, honey?"

"Pajamas?" Loni looked questionably at the doctor, and Dr. Morgan nodded her consent.

"She can wear her pajamas, and feel free to bring anything else you think will make her stay more comfortable."

"I'll bring some blankets and pillows too. Also some books and magazines. Do you want your sketchbook?"

"It's full, " Loni said with a chuckle. "Manny got me a new one, but I left it at the restaurant."

"I'll swing by and pick it up if Manny didn't already," Luca promised as he kissed her forehead.

"Is he here?" Loni asked with wide eyes cashing Kit to chuckle.

"Bright and early," Kit confirmed. "Should we send him in first?"

"I guess, but I look awful," the image of herself in the bathroom mirror this morning shocked her. She was so pale, and there were puffy blueish bags under her eyes.

"You look beautiful, and Manny will think so, too," Luca said, albeit begrudgingly. "We'll send him in."

She watched as her parents walked out with the doctor. They left her door open. She combed her hands through her hair nervously as she waited.

"Loni?" Manny's voice was timid as he carefully stepped into the room.

"Hey, come on in," she said as he stepped further in. He had a big bouquet with him and her gift bag from the night before.

"Manny, you didn't have to do that!" She exclaimed as he set the flowers on a table near her bedside.

"Wanted to," he quipped, setting the gift bag next to it. "I grabbed this from the restaurant last night too."

"Thank you," she offered as she turned to head to get a better look. "They are so pretty! So many roses."

"I remembered you saying roses were your favorite," he said as he went to sit in the chair at her bedside. "I got chocolates, too but the doctor said you can't have them yet."

"I haven't eaten anything in two days now, and I'm not even hungry; it's weird," she told him.

"How are you feeling?" He asked.

"About as bad as I look," she joked wryly.

"You always look pretty, Loni," Manny said as a blush touched his cheeks.

"Liar," she found herself blushing too, though.

"I'm so sorry about last night," she added after a moment. "That must've freaked you out."

"It did, but you have no reason to apologize!"

"I know, but still," she complained. "So, not how I wanted our first dance to end."

"Not what I had in mind either," Manny agreed. "Just glad you're okay."

"I'm not," she admitted quietly, "okay, I mean. They say my heart is failing."

"Damn, Loni," his green eyes filled with worry. "But they can fix it, right?"

"I don't know, she keeps saying they'll do everything they can, but she never says she can fix it."

"That's doctor talk, I think. They have to be careful, so they don't get sued."'

"Yeah, maybe," Loni said, "but it's all so scary sounding."

"Let's talk about something else then," he suggested.

"Good idea," she agreed, "what should we talk about?"

"Where would you be if you weren't here right now?"

"Probably painting," she mused. "Then I'd take my dog Lucky out for a walk. He always starts bugging me when I'm almost done, little troublemaker."

Manny laughed, "that's great. Do you ever take him to the dog park?"

"Sometimes. He loves running, but he's getting old, so we can't stay too long."

"When you leave here, maybe we can take him together?"

"I'd like that," she agreed with a smile tugging at her lips. "Would, um, that be like a date?"

"I'd love for it to be," he was grinning back at her.

That giddy, fluttery feeling erupted in her belly as her cheeks flushed.

"It might be a while before we can," she bit nervously at her lip. "I think I'll be stuck in here for a while."

"We'll just have to have a pretend date then."

"A pretend date?" She questioned.

"Yeah, when I was a kid, I got jealous when one of my friends got to go to Disney World. So my mom came up with this game where we pretended we went. Like imagining being there, it was fun. Something we kept doing through the years."

She frowned lightly; it seemed like Manny and his family struggled. Now it made sense why he had to sell his guitar.

"Don't feel bad about it." He seemed to sense her thoughts. "We had a lot of fun with it. Want to try it out?"

"Okay," Loni agreed. "So where should we go?"

"Anywhere you want! It's imaginary, so there are no limits."

"Umm.." she pondered. "There's a beautiful art gallery in Sun City; I've always wanted to go."

"Then that's where we're going," Manny said. "Ready?"

"Yup."

"I'm outside your door, all nervous to knock in case your dad kills me."

Loni laughed loudly. "Manny, it's a fantasy date. Why is my dad there?"

"Good point!" He agreed with a chuckle.

Loni's mood was lifting fast, a smile taking over her face.

"So, your parents aren't home. I knock, and you tell me to come on in and wait."

"I finish getting ready; I'm wearing a long pink silk gown, super fancy," she gushed. "My hair is down and all curly. I head to the stairway to meet you."

"My jaw is on the floor."

"Manny!" She giggled.

"Well, it is."

"What are you wearing?"

"Umm.." he pondered it for a moment. "Black pants and a nice button-down white shirt with a black tie, but skater sneakers to give it an edgy look."

"So hot! Now my jaw is on the floor," she quipped, making him laugh again. He was so right. This was fun!

"You're too sweet; all eyes will be on you anywhere we go."

"Stop!"

"You're beautiful, Loni," he said, their eyes locked.

"Thank you," the words came out as a whisper. Her belly danced with butterflies, but she knew it was all Manny this time and not her condition.

"Ready to go to Sun City?" He said after a moment, and she gulped as she nodded.

"We can drive my new car," she said gleefully.

"Or teleport and be there in seconds," Manny offered. "Fantasy date and all."

"Let's do that," she agreed with another giggle, and he suddenly took her hand. It sent a warmth through her skin and widened her smile. Their eyes met again, and a soft smile lit up Manny's handsome face.

"Close your eyes," he said as he did just that, and she joined. "Okay, ready? Open."

They both opened their eyes at the same time.

"We're in the middle of the sidewalk in sun city, a few blocks from the art gallery," Manny mused. "We're surrounded by big buildings with all these huge windows."

"The sidewalks are all cobblestone and lined with lush green glass," Loni added. "There are tons of people walking by us."

"I take your hand and bring you a little closer to me," he lowered his voice.

"I feel much warmer and safer when you do that," she whispered.

"Yeah?" His whole face lit up; he squeezed her hand a little. "We head into the gallery, and I step back so you can take the lead."

"It's amazing! Huge tall walls lined with beautiful artwork. My eyes don't even know where to look at first," she gushed, she could envision it so well, it almost did feel real. "I take a moment and enjoy feeling overwhelmed by art."

"I can't take my eyes off you; seeing and feeling your connection to the art around us is amazing."

"I finally bring you to a display of nature-inspired paintings that call to me."

"This is like what you like to paint the most right, nature and flowers?" Manny asked.

"Flowers are my biggest muse. I love painting them."

"I can't wait to see some of your artwork," Manny enthused. "I turn you around, so you see the big blank wall behind us. I could see this whole wall filled with your paintings."

"That would be so amazing," she breathed out. "I'd do my pink rose collection. This random bush in the center of all these red roses blooms beautiful pink roses once a year around my birthday."

"Wow, that's so special," Manny noted.

"I like to paint them in all their stages, from the leaves to the buds, the flowers as they bloom and then wilt and then the rosehip it leaves behind."

"Wow, Loni that sounds so cool."

"You think so?" She was bummed she didn't have her phone to show him some pictures. She'd have to ask someone about that soon.

"Yeah, you're the coolest girl I've ever met," he confessed as he squeezed her hand.

"Hardly!" She felt herself blushing as she giggled.

"Are you too, so where to next on our date?"

"You pick," she quipped.

"Okay, well, after we leave the museum, I see a horse carriage ahead and wave. They stop and let us on."

"Oh! This is romantic," she giggled again.

"You like it?" Manny was blushing a deep red.

"I do," Loni encouraged him and he relaxed.

Manny continued on then. "The horse trots along past all the buildings towards uptown. It's full of old-school Victorian-style mansions."

"I'm a little cold, so I scoot closer to you," Loni continued.

"I put a blanket over our laps and put my arm around you and ask if that's better."

"Much," she whispered.

"Good." Manny smiled his nervousness seemed to fading away more and more as they went on. "The buggy keeps moving and I point out some of the lit up mansions ahead."

She could almost feel his arm around her, if she needed a good reason to get better, making this date come true sure was it!

"I am wide eyed as I take it all in. I tell you I may even have to draw one of these houses while we're here," Loni continued, a dreamy tone to her voice, for a moment she could see the city instead of the stark white hospital room.

"I haven't looked at anything but you," Manny said quietly, sending a shiver through her body.

She raised her head to look at him and as their eyes locked, he leaned forward, and her heart started to flutter in her chest.

"This is where I'd tell you you're the most beautiful thing in this city," he leaned closer, his eyes dropped to her lips and then back to her eyes.

"And then you'd kiss me?" Her voice came out all breathy.

"First, I'd tell you I've wanted to kiss you all night."

"Then I'd ask what you were waiting for," she bit back a smile.

He lifted her hand and brought it to his lips, pressing a soft and slow kiss against the tender skin on the top of her hand. His warm lips sent a surge of warmth through her body.

"And then I'd kiss you," he said in a hoarse voice as he pulled his lips back from her hand.

She took a few breaths in and out to keep her heart calm as he gently lowered her hand. They smiled softly at each other.

"Loni?" Dr. Morgan popped in and glanced at them. "I want to check in on you, and I'd like you to meet some of the doctors on your team. So we'll have to ask your friend to leave, okay?"

"Can I see her again later?" Manny squeezed Loni's hand again before he stood up.

"Probably not today, but you can come back tomorrow," Dr. Morgan said. "I'll leave you two to say goodbye and be back in a few, Loni."

"I'll be back tomorrow, then," Manny said. "Text me if you get your phone back."

"I will," Loni promised.

"Thanks, Manny, for everything," she felt a lump of emotion for him. "That was the best date ever."

"It was a make-believe date," he chuckled. "But it was pretty epic, wasn't it?"

"Yes! Can we have another one soon?"

"Anytime you want," Manny agreed, "and we can go anywhere too. So you'll have to think of some cool places."

"Want to know a secret?"

"What?"

"That was my first date," she confessed.

"Yeah?" He looked a little surprised, but it lit his eyes up. "Mine too."

"No way!"

"Way!" He laughed lightly, "I hope I described it all right."

"It was perfect," she said dreamily.

Manny brought a hand to her cheek and rested it there. "I'll see you later, Loni. Take care, okay, and rest up."

"I will. Bye, Manny."

"So epic," she said to herself; after he left, her cheeks were sore from grinning.

Chapter 8

"How does this look? Is it crooked?" Kit looked over at Loni and Carly, who was sitting on on the edge of her hospital bed. "Can you see it okay from there?"

"I can see it fine, mom," Loni assured her. "It looks great!"

After Manny left, Loni slept most of the afternoon but was woken up when her mom and dad returned from Lissa's testing.

Kit had brought a handful of Loni's paintings and drawings and hung them around her hospital room. In addition, she had packed a duffel bag and brought over some better blankets and pillows for Loni's room and the on-call room.

She'd been fretting over what to hang up where for nearly an hour now. Loni knew it was to distract herself, though. Both her mom and dad had been on edge since Lissa's test this afternoon. They were very impatiently waiting for the results. Luca had nearly burned a hole in the floor pacing, and it was a hard hospital floor! Andre had convinced him to take a walk with him a while ago.

"Oh, a purple daisy! That's pretty!" Carly noted as Kit hung the next picture on the wall.

"It's called an Aster Celeste. It's considered a wildflower, but some find it a nuisance because it can take over. Grows almost like a weed," Loni explained.

"How do you know so much about this stuff?" Carly looked impressed.

"She's always been obsessed with flowers." Kit smiled softly. "That's all she ever wanted for birthdays was art stuff or books on flowers."

"I painted that recently. I had a dream about that flower," Loni recalled. "A whole field of them among other wildflowers. It was beautiful. I had to look up what they were when I woke up."

"And then you had to paint it," Carly smiled fondly.

"Exactly," Loni agreed.

"That is strange you dreamed that. There are no wildflower fields near us," Kit mused.

"I know," Loni said, "must've just been something I saw once, maybe when we drove somewhere and forgot about."

"Must've," Kit agreed. "Speaking of flowers, Manny picked out a nice arrangement."

"He's got a great eye." Loni looked wistfully at the beautiful bouquet.

"So, tell us about his visit?" Carly prodded with a little giggle. "He was beaming when he walked out of the room."

Loni blushed as a grin curled over her lips. She wanted to keep their little fantasy date a secret for now. It just felt more special that way.

"It was good; he's so cute and we had a lot of fun talking," Loni gushed.

"More 'deets than that!" Carly mock scolded her.

"Nope, that's all I'm giving up," Loni giggled.

"He is such a sweet boy," Kit told her, "don't tell your dad I told you this, but even he likes Manny."

"I knew it!" Loni exclaimed.

"He was really impressed that Manny was here right away this morning," Carly added.

"That's what he wants, what we both want for you, someone that cares and shows it."

"He does," Loni smiled. "...Are guitars expensive?"

"I think so," Kit said, "I've never bought one, but I assume. Why?"

"Manny said he had to sell his. He said he would get a new one someday, but then he got me that sketchbook and those flowers and I feel bad. I don't want to set him back."

"It's more expensive than a sketch book, hon. I don't think you set him back much," Carly assured her.

"Why'd he have to sell his guitar?" Kit asked.

"He didn't say."'

"Well, maybe I can talk to dad about giving him a little raise or something." Kit started rummaging through the bag she had brought. "Do you want Carly and I to help you get into your pajamas?"

"Yes! Please!" Loni said eagerly. "This hospital gown is so awful. Do you think I can shower soon?"

"We'll ask Dr. Morgan about that later," Kit said.

Loni assumed it would be an ordeal like whenever she had to pee; the nurses had to come in and ensure she didn't unhook any machines.

Kit used the remote to lift the bed as Carly went to shut Loni's hospital door. Loni sat up carefully with the help of Kit, and soon Carly rushed back over to help keep her steady as well. Lying as much as she did make standing even harder; she was always wobbly.

"Your ankles!" Carly cried out, seeing how swollen Loni's ankles were. They were double the size. Loni and her parents had flipped out over them earlier that morning.

"Woke up like that; Dr. Morgan said retaining water is normal, I guess," Loni explained.

Kit sighed, "Nothing about this is normal."

Kit helped Loni slide her hospital gown off and then Carly helped her into the shirt while Kit hoisted up the pants. She never thought at sixteen she'd need help getting dressed.

She was breathing hard as they finished and got her settled back into her bed.

"You okay?" Kit oversaw her as Loni breathed in and out slowly like Dr. Morgan told her; soon enough, she caught her breath again.

"Yeah, I'm okay," Loni promised. "But I'm exhausted now."

No sooner had she said it, then a yawn slipped out.

"Why don't we check on Luca and Andre and let her rest?" Carly suggested to Kit.

She stood for another moment studying Loni. "We'll be back in soon, honey."

"Okay, mom," Loni said, already drifting off.

"Do you want Carly and I to take Lissa tonight? We're taking the twins to a movie to get their mind off stuff. Might be nice for Lissa too." Andre asked as he and Luca returned to the cardiology wing.

"Yeah...as long as her results are okay," Luca was counting hard on this thing being rare. It couldn't affect both of his girls. It just couldn't. That would be beyond cruel...this was already so brutal.

Life isn't always easy. Sometimes it can be brutal, but if you two hold on to each other, you'll get through it, all of it.

His dad had no idea how true they could be when he wrote those words. Luca wasn't sure how he was holding up, Kit either, but he was confident his dad was somehow helping them find the strength.

They found Lissa playing cards with Stone in the waiting room. Loni's friends had left earlier when Dr. Morgan limited visitors to family for the rest of the day.

Kit and Carly left Loni's room just as Dr. Morgan excited her office with paperwork.

"Are they"-

"Results are in," she cut him off.

"Am I okay? Do I have brahmana?" Lissa stood up anxiously.

"Brugada," Dr. Morgan corrected her with a warm smile.

She gestured for them to follow her into her office. A few doctors huddled around a table, going over scans and paperwork. One of them glanced over when they came in, his eyes landing on Kit. When he felt Luca's curious gaze, he quickly looked away. It didn't seem like he was checking her out, but it felt weird. Now wasn't the time to puff his chest out, though, so he ignored it.

"Everything came back negative for Lissa," Dr. Morgan said to Luca's immense relief.

"Oh, thank god, thank you," Kit said tearfully as she started to collapse. Luca quickly wrapped his arms around her, his eyes filling with the same grateful tears as hers.

"You're sure? " Luca asked.

"Her heart is in great shape. However, I still want to test her regularly."

"Why Loni and not me? It's not fair," Lissa asked the doctor.

"Unfortunately, conditions like this, don't play fair."

"Still, if anyone should be sick, it should be me. I'm the one always causing trouble."

Luca felt his heart shatter; before he could speak, Kit had already pulled away and kneeled in front of Lissa.

"No.." Kit told her slowly, "don't you ever think that. Do you hear me? I'd never wish for this for either of you in a million, trillion, billion years."

"But it should have been me. Not Loni. She doesn't deserve this. She doesn't do anything wrong. She's the perfect one! Why her!?"

"We don't know why her. We may never know. But you are just as perfect as Loni. Loni would never want you to wish this for yourself, and we don't either," Kit said firmly. "Are you a little more challenging, behavior-wise, than Loni, sure? But you know what else you are?"

"What?" Lissa sniffled back tears.

"You're spunky, brilliant, and hilarious. You're full of life at all times. You remind us every day to live for the moment. You've been our little miss personality since you were just a baby, and we wouldn't have it any other way."

Lissa was starting to cry, and so was Luca. His wife always had the right words at the right moment.

"We love you each for exactly who you are," Kit continued. "You, Lissa, make us laugh daily with your little antics. You're just like your dad, and you know how much I love your dad, right?"

"Yeah, it's pretty disgusting."

Everyone in the room chuckled at that. "Let's give them a moment." Dr. Morgan said she motioned for the other doctors, and they followed him out, closing the door behind him.

"See, shorty?" Luca managed to get a hold of his emotions and knelt next to Kit. "In the worst moment, you can make everyone laugh. They call you a mini-me, and you are a lot like me. What people don't know, though, is some of that humor is sometimes a defensive thing, huh?"

"Yeah," she confessed in a low voice.

"Yeah, I know. Another thing we have in common is that perfect sibling. Andre was younger than me, but he was just like my dad. Driven, motivated, and well-mannered. People used to say, why can't you behave better like your brother."

"That must've been super annoying."

"It was," Luca agreed. "And it caused us to bicker and stuff. My dad and I also had some issues I won't get into now, which caused tension too."

Lissa quietly listened, her tears subsiding as she took it all in.

"I realized later in life that we both had our good things and our faults. I'm so glad we're best friends now, and I don't want you and Loni ever to feel bitter toward each other. Not ever."

"He's right, baby." Kit chimed in. "Your sisters and you need each other. Now more than ever. You can't feel guilty that she has it and you don't, be grateful, because now you have more energy for her. She's going to need that."

"I will keep her spirits up, whatever she needs I'll be there," Lissa agreed.

"Come here." Luca pulled her and Kit into a group hug and the trio sat on Dr. Morgan's office floor, comforting each other.

The hospital went silent after nine. Carly and Andre did take a reluctant Lissa with them for the night. She only left because Loni insisted she needed to ensure Lucky was okay. They'd found Loni's phone in her car that morning, and she sent it home with Lissa so her sister could take pictures of Lucky and the roses for her.

Luca and Kit sat with Loni, who'd fallen asleep a few minutes earlier. They were both reluctant to leave her room for the on-call room and were putting it off.

Luca's phone sounded, and he frowned as he looked at the screen.

"What is it, babe?" Kit asked nervously.

"It's the alarm for the restaurant," Luca murmured.

"What?" Kit frowned, "someone broke in?"

"I'm sure it's nothing, but I'm going to go check it out to be safe."

"Luca!" She stood up and then winced when Loni mumbled, luckily she didn't wake. "You can't go alone," she said in a quieter voice.

"Kit Kat, if anything, it's some teenagers."

"Please just call my dad to go with you," she begged.

"Okay," he promised her holding up his phone, "I'll call him on the way."

"Thank you," she breathed. "With Loni...I'm just on edge."

"I know baby, me too," he kissed her forehead. "I'll be back soon. I love you."

"Love you too."

The drive to the restaurant only took five minutes. Stone was still closing up the Willow Grill, the bar he worked at down the road from Leo's, but said he'd meet him soon.

Luca pulled in and saw an old beat-up red car, and next to it, he instantly recognized a blue dodge as Manny's.

"Manny?" With a frown, Luca got out of the car. He peered into the windows of the red car and noticed a lot of stuff in it.

As he headed inside, Manny stood at the bar, and his eyes widened in horror when he saw Luca.

"Manny? What are you doing here at this time? What's going on?" Luca could sense the fear coming off the kid and tried to keep his tone light.

"It's my fault! Mr. Donato, please don't blame my son." A woman came from the bathroom; her dark black hair was wet and her brown eyes was sorrowful as she drew closer.

"I have a job interview tomorrow and needed to freshen up. I convinced him to let me use the bathroom here. I promise we didn't take a thing, we never would."

Luca was taken aback as his eyes shifted from Manny to the woman. He had no clue Manny had it this bad.

"Manny," Luca said calmly. "Can you go in the kitchen? All that food from Loni's party is just sitting there in the walk-in. Go heat up a bunch of it."

"We couldn't eat your food!" She shook her head.

"It'll just go to waste otherwise, please," Luca pressed but gently, and she nodded at Manny to go ahead.

"I am sorry, Mr. Donato."

"Please call me Luca, and you don't need to apologize. Ms. Ramirez."

"Call me, Ava, please," she offered. "And I do want to apologize because it breached your trust, which means a lot to my son. He cares very much for your daughter and looks up to you. This job has been such a blessing for us."

"I accept your apology, but coming in to use the bathroom is fine, really, " Luca assured her.

"If I can get this job, I can turn things around for Manny and me."

"You're homeless?" Luca asked softly.

"Recently," she confirmed, a weary look in her eyes. "I was fired a year ago and struggled to find work. We moved here when I was offered a job at the shoe factory right outside of town. I thought it was a new start for us here. I found a small house to rent, and the town is safe and beautiful compared to the city."

She paused for a moment, the pain in her eyes evident.

"But someone decided the shoe factory was spending too much money on labor, and they ended up laying off most of the new hires myself included. We tried hard to keep up with the rent. I'm ashamed to admit I had to take most of Manny's earnings to get us by. He wanted to help, but it still kills me. Finally it became too much, and we got too far behind. We have been staying in our cars, or at the shelter, for a week or so now. Manny hates the shelter he's afraid if the school kids see him there.."

"Right," Luca nodded with a sad sigh, kids were cruel they'd tease him for it and make high school miserable for the kid. "Is it too late to back-pay the rent? I can help. My brother has attorney connections, and we have plenty of savings.."

"I couldn't possibly take your money, Luca," she said in a slightly clipped tone.

"Look, I understand, but you know why we have this place and the money in the bank?"

She tilted her head slightly, "why?"

"My dad gave it to us, and his words were, not to spoil us but to make sure we had the time we needed to build memories, and didn't have to work all the time. This place was to continue his legacy and it did so well, we never needed most of the money he left. If he was here now this is exactly what he'd want, to help someone with it."

"I do appreciate the gesture, but I just can't. Your child is in the hospital. There is no telling how much the medical bills could amount to. You can't have this place open while you worry about her and that will drain the bills. You will need that money."

"You can't live in your car with a kid, either," Luca countered.

"Whoa." Luca turned to see Stone had come in. He was gaping at Ava and then looked at Luca with confusion. "What's going on? Whose living in a car?"

"Hey, dad, this is Manny's mom, Ava," Luca introduced the two. "This is my wife Kit's dad, Stone."

Stone held his hand out and shook hers. "You and Manny need help?"

"We'll be okay. I have an interview tomorrow. It'll all turn around then." She looked like she was trying to convince herself.

"You'll do great, mom; I know you will." Manny had returned with two large platters of heated pasta.

For the first time since Loni collapsed, Luca felt a pang of hunger. He sent a text to Kit so she wouldn't worry but opted to take ten to figure this out and have some food. Manny started dishing them up while Luca grabbed some forks from behind the bar and filled them each a water.

Manny started digging right in, and Luca saw the kid was starving. He'd probably spent his food money on Loni's flowers and the donuts he brought in that morning.

"Listen, Ava. If you don't get that job, I can always use some help at the Grill," Stone offered. "Especially now. I can't be there much with Loni and all."

"That would be amazing. I have a lot of restaurant experience," she perked up at Stone's offer.

"If this is an overstep, you can smack me, but I got a big empty house with two empty bedrooms. You and Manny can stay with me if you want." Stone offered before digging into his food.

Luca was surprised at the gesture, but Stone had been alone for some time in that house. Kit often worried he got lonely.

"I couldn't... we couldn't impose," she said, but her tone was hesitant.

"Do you clean?" Stone asked her.

"Of course."

"Then it wouldn't be an imposition," Luca said. "He won't clean, and my wife has to go over there and do it for him."

"You make your daughter come clean your house?" She asked with a chuckle.

Stone shrugged, "she chooses to. I'd be fine with a little dust."

"Well, if it would help your family during this time.." she was slowly considering it, and Manny was lighting up at the idea. Poor kid, Luca couldn't imagine sleeping in a car at sixteen.

"I'd want to pay rent once I'm working," Ava said.

"I don't need it," Stone said. "Mortgage is paid for. Just take the time to save up. Get you and Manny someplace better."

"Mom, I think we should take this," Manny said. His entire bowl of pasta was gone, Luca scooped him a second.

"I just don't want to feel like a burden. I've always paid our way." Ava frowned, but her gaze softened at Manny's hopeful expression.

"I'd be the burden." Stone smirked, "I'm not a picnic to live with. I'm messy. I smoke weed and I keep odd hours. But if you don't mind all that, and can help with cleaning. Why not?"

"I have a son to consider. I have to set my pride aside and accept this," she sighed wearily. "Thank you, we will give this is a try but I insist on helping as much as I can."

"My daughter, my nephew and me, were in a tough place when Luca got to town. When his old man passed on he took care of all of us, and I think he'd like us to take care of other people, you know?"

Ava smiled. "Your son in law said something similar and I do like that sentiment."

"Well Manny you got a new roomie," Stone flashed him a grin and Manny returned it.

"Don't you dare offer my son any weed," Ava warned him.

Stone's smirk widened. "I'll only offer it to you then."

She rolled her eyes, "I'm going to regret this, aren't I?"

"Yeah, probably," Luca chuckled as he stood up. "But he knows better then that, don't worry."

"I only encourage tattoos," Stone agreed.

"No tattoos either," Ava said warningly looking at Manny.

"Ah this should be fun," Stone looked amused and Ava glared at him. Luca chuckled lightly as he stood up.

"I better get back to Loni. Can you all lock up?" Luca asked as he ducked behind the bar to fill a To-go box of pasta for Kit, she kept asking when everyone else had eaten but hadn't eaten a thing in days herself.

"Yeah, we got it," Stone promised.

"Thanks," Luca said as he ducked out.

As he headed towards his car, Manny's voice stopped him.

"Luca, wait."

"What's up, Manny?" Luca asked.

"I'm sorry again that we just came in like this."

"It's okay. I'm not mad about you and mom being here tonight. But, in the future, if you ever need help, let me know, okay?"

"Okay," he agreed. "I felt sort of embarrassed. I tried hard to help my mom, and it wasn't enough."

"You have nothing to be embarrassed about. Life can be shitty but you stood up and did what you could to help. I'm proud of you," Luca squeezed his shoulder. "Go on in and lock up. I doubt Stone has any food, so bring home whatever is left from that party."

"Thank you, Luca," Manny gulped, "for everything."

"No, thank you, kid. You make my little girl smile, and right now, that's everything."

Chapter 9

"A penny for my thoughts? Oh no, I'll sell em for a dollar. They're worth so much more after I'm a goner."

"That one looks like a boat!"

"A boat? I see a dragon."

"A dragon?"

The sound of London's sweet laughter filled the air; year thirteen, a big one, a milestone, as they say.

"Don't you see it? There are the horns, and that's the smoke he's breathing out." London pointed to the slow-moving cloud they were contemplating.

The mother had the luxury of getting the entire day with London. She intended to enjoy every moment of it. Yet as she gazed at her daughter's maturing face, those melancholy thoughts slipped in as always.

"Mom, tell me why you always get so sad on my birthday." London turned her head to gaze into her eyes.

Curiosity burned through those honey browns. Sometimes, she worried London could pull the truth right out of her with those knowing eyes of hers.

"I told you, sweetheart. It's because you're growing up, and it makes me sad."

"I think there's more to it," London argued.

"There isn't. Let's just enjoy the day."

"But mom"-

"Look, London, that one looks like a rose." She pointed to a new cloud floating over their heads.

"I hope the rose bushes come back next year," London said dreamily.

The purple daisy-like flowers had taken over the field again, some other wildflowers remained. But the rose bushes were one of the flowers they overtook.

They fell silent as they laid there, watching the clouds float slowly above them.

The horrible shrill ringing of a cell phone broke up the peaceful moment.

"Mom, aren't you going to answer that?" London asked.

"No, I don't want to waste a second of this special day talking to anyone but you."

"What if it's important, though?"

"Whatever it is can wait."

"Come on, pick up," a frustrated plea woke Loni up. She opened her eyes to see one of the doctors on her team, Dr. Blake, sighing as he shoved a phone into his pocket.

"Busted," Loni teased, and he cracked a soft smile at her.

"Sorry, I didn't mean to wake you."

"It's okay," she said, "all I do is sleep anyway."

"I heard you got to take a shower last night," Dr. Blake offered. "That's something."

"Yay, me," she said dryly.

"Find some happiness in the normal things even if they seem like nothing. It'll help keep your spirits up." He walked over to check her vitals.

"Dr. Morgan said I should try to eat a little something today."

"I bet that'll help," he jotted some things down on a clipboard, and there was a flicker of concern in his eyes.

"I'm getting worse, aren't I?" Loni asked as she looked up and met his gaze. "I can tell, your eyes, they look...worried."

"My mom always said my eyes give everything away," Dr. Blake cringed. "I should get better at my poker face."

Despite not having a poker face, he did have nice eyes, brown sort of like her own, only a darker shade. He was good-looking, with wavy ashy brown hair and a dash of freckles across his nose.

"So I am, then? Getting worse?"

"The beta blockers can make things worse before they get better," he said slowly and carefully. "It's too soon to say they're not working. The next twenty-four hours are going to be telling."

"What if they don't work?"

"Let's not get ahead of ourselves," he said. "I know you're tired of hearing this, but don't dwell on what's going on all the time. Try and think about other things."

"I know," she agreed with a sigh. "I am trying to keep my mind off it."

"Think about the sugar-free jello and bland turkey sandwich you'll get to eat later," Dr. Blake joked.

"Can't wait," she giggled. "It's weird. Food is the one thing I like as much as flowers and painting, and I have zero desire for it. My mom was eating my favorite pasta last night, and I didn't even want a bite of it."

"What kind of pasta?"

"Penne with Rosa sauce. My dad's specialty. Well, one of them," she bragged. "He's an amazing chef."

"Yum. I prefer a carbonara myself, but that sounds good."

"That's heavy for a doctor!"

"Little secret," he leaned in and gave her a conspiratorial wink. "Doctors aren't always beacons of health. Actually, we can be awful to our own bodies. A bunch of hypocrites is what we are."

Loni laughed at that, "your secret is safe with me, I promise."

"So you like panting flowers?" He looked at her walls with a wistful smile. "You're very talented."

"Thank you! It's always been an obsession of mine. I started by coloring our rose bushes when I was just a kid and never stopped."

"My sister started getting into art at a young age too. Flowers inspired her too. Actually, they were one of the only things she ever drew."

"Oh yeah? I do some other stuff. I did some food for my family's restaurant, a bunch or our dog Lucky, and some other nature stuff. I like flowers the most, though."

"So what is about them? The colors or..?"

"Flowers are the prettiest things on earth, yet they don't disturb anyone. They exist and make us happy just by being," Loni mused. "But they die so fast; it's not fair. I feel like by painting them; I elongate their life."

"That's beautiful," he sounded a little choked up. His eyes landed on the Aster Celeste she'd done recently, and he stared at it for a long moment.

"Are you okay, Dr. Blake?"

"Just fine," he quickly regrouped. "I better get your results over to Dr. Morgan. She'll be in to check on you later."

"Can I have visitors today?"

"Sure, but if you get tired, kick 'em out, doctors orders."

"Okay Dr. Blake," she agreed.

Out of all her doctors he was her favorite so far, she really liked him.

"You get any sleep last night?" Luca asked with a tired yawn as Kit pulled her damp locks into a ponytail for the day. The small on-call room luckily came with an attached bathroom and shower.

"Maybe a little," she stifled her own yawn.

Neither of them liked being even two doors down from Loni at night. The heart attack in her sleep was haunting them both, even though Dr. Morgan had assured them at least once doctor from her team was always on standby, in or near Loni's room.

Manny's family problems had been a big topic to focus on last night, even though Kit felt awful for him. It was a nice reprieve to think about something else for a little bit, anyhow.

They didn't want to worry Loni too much, so they told her that Manny's mom was having some recent trouble and they would be staying with Stone for a while. They left out the part about Manny having been sleeping in his car. That poor boy, Kit wished they'd known he needed help sooner.

She and Luca stepped out of the on-call room into the waiting area. The elevator opened, revealing Lissa along with Stone and Manny.

"Hi, mom and daddio. Is Loni up yet?"

"We haven't been in yet. I thought you'd be coming in with your aunt and uncle today?" Kit questioned.

"She insisted I pick her up this morning," Stone explained. "Carly and Andre are taking the twins to her mom's but will be by later."

"Carly needs to get them tested," Kit said worriedly as she glanced at Luca.

"Andre said they set something up for the end of the week," Luca assured her.

"Have you had breakfast?" Kit asked Lissa, who shook her head no.

Luca grabbed some bills from his wallet and handed them to Manny. "Can you take her to the cafeteria and get you both something to eat?"

"You don't have to"-

"Just take it and get some food, kid," Luca said as he ruffled his hair.

"Thanks, Luca," he said sheepishly.

"Race you!" Lissa took off in a run, and Manny rolled his eyes as he followed her.

"So, how's it going so far with the new roommates?" Kit asked Stone.

"Okay, I guess," he said with a shrug. "Ava's making me smoke outside, though."

"What?" Luca questioned like he heard him wrong.

"And you listened to her?" Kit was stunned.

"She shamed me!"

"Shamed you?" Luca tilted his head for clarification.

"Yeah, she said if I want to destroy my heart and lungs, knowing what's happening to my granddaughter, that's my choice, but she and Manny deserve clean air." He huffed at that and plopped down into a chair.

"She's not wrong," Luca commented.

"I like her," Kit declared.

"Of course you do," Stone muttered.

"Speaking of Manny, I need a little favor, dad," Luca said.

"What's that?" Stone asked.

"Can you find out what kind of guitar he likes?"

"Yeah, sure; why, though?"

"He sold his to cover rent; let's get the kid a new one, huh?"

"Agreed," Stone said, "I'm on it."

The elevator opened again, and Cathy and Andrea came out this time.

"Morning," Cathy said as Andrea went to sit down. "How is Loni doing?"

"Can I see her today?" Andrea asked.

"We're going to head in right now to check on her, and we'll be back out to let you know," Kit promised.

She took Luca's hand, and they walked into Loni's room. She was awake and looked up with a smile as they came in.

"Morning, honey," Kit said as she made her way over to her bedside.

"You're popular this morning," Luca told her. "Andrea and Manny are both already here to see you."

"They said I can have visitors as long as I'm not tired," Loni's eyes lit up. "I'm going to try eating today too."

"Does that mean you're feeling better?" Luca asked, and her eyes dimmed some.

"Not really, but maybe food will help?"

"Only one to way to find out," Dr. Morgan entered with a tray.

Kit grabbed the remote and raised her bed for her; she then slid her beside the table to be used as a ledge to eat off of.

"No turkey sandwich and jello?" Loni asked as she eyed the oatmeal and hard-boiled egg.

"That's lunch later," Dr. Morgan explained. "I'd rather we try food earlier in the day. This condition tends to be best in the morning and worsens as the day progresses."

Loni grabbed the spoon and took a bite as Dr. Morgan jotted a few things down on her chart.

"How is it?" Luca asked.

"Terrible," Loni confessed as she wrinkled her nose at it.

"Sorry, we have to limit your sugar, so it's plain," Dr. Morgan explained.

"It's okay; I'll just pretend it's chocolate chip pancakes," Loni offered.

"Good luck with that," Luca quipped.

"With enough imagination, it works," Loni closed her eyes as she took her next bite. "I can almost taste the melty chocolate now."

Dr. Morgan chuckled softly, "enjoy. I'll be in again to check on you soon."

She ate a little more and then pushed the bowl away. She took a few bites of the egg, which Kit guessed had no salt based on her grimace.

"That's all I can manage. Imagination works better for dates than food." Loni said.

"What?" Luca questioned.

"Never mind!" She blushed hard.

Kit made a mental note to ask her more about that later when Luca was preoccupied.

"Can I see Manny now?" Loni asked as Kit pushed the table back to her bedside, and a nurse came to dispose of her tray.

"What's wrong with us? Getting bored of our company?" Luca teased with a smirk tugging at his lips.

"I think you two should go and get some breakfast." Loni gave Luca a stern look. "You heard Dr. Morgan. Take care of yourselves too."

"We had dinner last night," Kit offered feebly, causing Loni to give her a hard look next, reminding Kit so much of herself that she couldn't help but laugh softly.

"Go eat," Loni urged.

"Why don't I send Andrea in first?" Kit asked. "She was sad when she didn't see you yesterday."

"Okay," Loni agreed as she sat up some.

"We'll be in the cafeteria and be back in soon." Luca kissed her forehead, and Kit squeezed her shoulder before they headed out.

Loni took a small sip of water while she waited for Andrea, her belly felt uneasy with the food in it, but the water helped some.

Andrea stepped in and looked a little nervous as she slowly approached. She was dressed down in a pair of leggings and an oversized tee shirt. Her dark hair was pulled into a loose bun.

"It's okay; I'm not going to keel over on you, don't worry," Loni assured her.

"I heard my mom say you're heart is failing?" Andrea looked bewildered that she came to sit by Loni's bed in one of the chairs.

"Yeah. I know it sounds so crazy," Loni said.

"Are they going to fix it? How? Does that mean your heart could just stop beating?"

"They are trying something called a beta blocker, they have a whole team here trying to fix me, and yeah, it could stop. It could also beat too hard and send me into cardiac arrest."

"My gosh, Loni, that is so scary!"

"I know, but all these machines keep it going, I guess," Loni tried to sound assuring. "They keep telling me to keep my mind off it."

"Makes sense," Andrea looked like she wanted to ask more but didn't. "So .. Manny was here super early this morning too."

"He was yesterday, too," Loni felt herself blushing.

"I know I saw, and I saw the flowers. That's so sweet, Loni!" Andrea gushed. "You know he really likes you if he's here even now."

Loni frowned at that. "What do you mean?"

"I mean, guys hate drama," Andrea said. "They just want someone to go to parties with, flirt, text, and make out with. So if he's here during all this, it's a good sign he really likes you."

"Not all guys are like that," Loni corrected her.

"Most are. Manny is a rare one."

"No, he's not," Loni argued. "I mean, he is... rare, but there are other guys that are genuine and not just about parties and stuff. What about Jamal? He's liked you forever, and he is so nice."

"All he ever wants to do is read or talk about reading," Andrea sighed.

"That used to be your favorite thing to do, too, remember?"

"I know, but Kelly says that's super lame."

"Kelly is super lame," Loni blurted out.

"She is not. She's the most popular girl in school."

"I know, but why? What's so interesting about her anyway? I mean, sure, she's really pretty, but all she ever talks about is clothes and hair."

"Not always, and she is my friend too, you know. You shouldn't talk bad about her," Andrea scolded.

"I'm not meaning to, I just," Loni considered her words carefully. "Sometimes I feel like she's changed you. If she were a good friend, she wouldn't run down the things you like, like reading and writing."

"Where is all this coming from?" Andrea's eyes darkened some, and she frowned.

"I've wanted to say it for a while, but... I don't know," Loni confessed. "I guess I was afraid you'd get mad."

"I'm not mad, but it's not like that. I am over reading and all that nerdy stuff. It's not just for Kelly," Andrea said defensively. "People can change."

"Okay... I'm sorry I talked bad about Kelly then," Loni said softly. "As long as you know, there's nothing lame about reading."

"Of course, I'm just over it is all," Andrea said in a fake chipper voice.

Loni didn't believe her one bit. Their whole lives, Andrea's head was buried in a book. She didn't want to push her too much, though, bad enough; she was already slipping away.

She was about to change the subject when her stomach started to churn and badly.

"Andrea - I'm going to"- before she could finish the sentence, her breakfast came up violently.

Andrea gasped and jumped away as Loni continued to puke her guts out. Her clean pajamas, blanket, and even her hair were all full of throw-up when she was done.

Tears started to rain down Loni's face; she couldn't help it.

"Loni, are you okay? I'll go get the doctor!" Andrea didn't need to, as several nurses and a few doctors rushed into the room. Andrea ducked out in a hurry as they ran in.

A nurse sat her up slightly and gave her a bucket in case she had to throw up again. Meanwhile, the doctors were checking her vitals.

"What happened!?" Kit cried out as she and Luca ran into the room.

"Her vitals are okay; she just couldn't keep the food down," one of the doctors assured her.

"I'm a big mess now," Loni sniffled as tears ran down her cheeks.

"Shh," Luca was at her bedside in seconds, pulling her puked-up self into his arms. "It's okay, pumpkin. We'll get you cleaned up."

Kit was already rummaging through her bag for fresh pajamas.

"I didn't even get to see Manny yet, and now I'm all gross," she sobbed into her dad's chest as he stroked her hair.

"You're okay," Luca said soothingly.

"But I'm not, I'm not okay," Loni cried, "and I'm getting worse."

"Oh, sweetheart," Kit came to sit on the other side of her, her hand gently stroking Loni's back as Luca held her.

"This isn't fair! It's so unfair," Loni sobbed.

She wasn't crying over the throw-up or even Manny anymore.

It was everything, all of it. The dam had broken, and she let it all out as her parents held her.

Chapter 10

"Gather up your tears and keep em in your pocket. Save 'em for a time when you're really gonna need 'em."

Year fifteen was another shared day. The mother sat patiently as she waited, and soon enough, the little blue car pulled up alongside the edge of the field. Her smile wavered when her ex-husband exited the passenger seat and not London. He waved briefly, and then the driver's door opened, and an excited London climbed out all smiles as she hugged her dad goodbye.

Driving? No! How could he?

Too soon, far too soon.

"Mom!" London cried out as she ran through the field of mostly purple flowers, her long red hair whipping over her face from the win.

"Hi, Sweetheart." She pulled back slightly to peer at her daughter; she was maturing so much, becoming such a beautiful young woman. "Dad is letting you drive?"

"Mom," London groaned as she pulled away. "I'm fifteen now. I'm going to be getting my learner's permit."

"But you don't have it yet."

"Close enough," London huffed as she plopped down with her sketch pad.

The mother bit her tongue. She couldn't argue this if her dad was already letting her do it. He'd let their son start driving even younger...also without running it by her first.

She sat beside London, slower, as her knees couldn't handle an ungraceful plop these days.

"My goodness, look at that sketch; it's incredible," she looked over London's shoulder. London had filled the entire page with various flowers of all different colors and styles but had done it abstractly, all the flowers blurring into each other in incredible ways. Her talent was extraordinary.

"You like it? It's every flower I've ever seen," London said dreamily as she looked at the page.

"I love it, sweetheart. You are so incredibly talented I couldn't be prouder of you."

"Mom," her tone had a nervous edge to it.

"What is it?"

"You're not the only one that thinks that," London said carefully.

"Well, of course, I'm not. Anyone that would see your drawings would think the same."

"Well, my art teacher, Ms. Munson, did, and she uh, she sent one of my drawings to the Madison Art Academy. They... they loved it."

"Isn't that school out in New Haven? That's across the country."

"I know." London but her lip. "And I got in."

"Got in? You're just a freshman in high school."

"They have a special program for sixteen to eighteen-year-olds, it's during the summer only, but any credits would go toward the college program when I start. But besides that, the experience would be invaluable to me."

"I... when would this start?"

"Next summer," London said. "Mom, please. Please say yes."

"This school is probably costly...."

"Dad said he would pay for it."

Of course, he did... Couldn't he take five minutes to call her before telling the kids whatever they wanted to hear? Why did he always have to make her the bad guy?

"London, you're too young to spend a summer so far away from us."

The idea of London so many miles away struck her heart with cold and slightly irrational fears. She wasn't ready for all this; she thought she had at least another year before London started talking about college and moving away.

"I'll be sixteen then!"

"Sixteen is too young, sweetheart, I'm sorry, but art school can wait until you're done with high school."

"Mom, they don't offer this to just anyone; this is huge!"

"You're only sixteen once. Why not enjoy next summer with your friends? "

Silence. Nothing but a sulking redhead next to her.

"Maybe you'll even meet a boy?" She offered with a teasing nudge.

"Whatever," London muttered.

The mood set in and dampened the day, an uneasy silence falling over mother and daughter. She had a bad feeling this wasn't the first and was far from the last fight over this topic.

Mentally she prepared herself for year fifteen...

Kit sat quietly, watching Loni as she slept; Luca was passed out in the chair on the other side of her. It had been a long and rough day; after Loni had her breakdown and they cleaned her up, she passed out from exhaustion. She'd woken up a few times, but not for very long. She had been taking this all so well and gracefully until today; a breakdown was long overdue. Seeing Loni like that was the hardest thing yet though, it was devastating knowing what she was going through.

"Mom?" Loni's hoarse voice came as she lifted her weary eyes open; she looked so pale and puffy.

"Hi honey," Kit crossed the room and sat at her bedside; there was no point in asking how she was feeling; it was obvious that Loni felt terrible, and Kit felt so helpless.

"Dad's finally asleep," Loni nodded toward Luca, who let out a loud snore as an answer making both of them giggle.

"Finally," Kit whispered. "He needs it."

"I bet," Loni agreed.

"While he's sleeping, what's all this about imaginary dates?"

Loni blushed, and a tiny smile curled on her lips; it was everything after seeing her devastation earlier to see even a small smile.

"So, Manny said he and his mom used to do pretend trips like to Disney World and stuff like that. So we thought going on a pretend date would be fun."

"That's adorable! Where did he pretend to take you?"

"To an art gallery in Sun City and then a carriage ride there."

"Oh, he's good; that's almost as smooth as your dad."

"Mom, don't use the word smooth." Loni crinkled her nose, and Kit laughed.

"What's wrong with smooth?"

"It sounds weird; it's creeping me out." Loni did a mock shudder.

Kit felt a little better, seeing Loni was getting back to herself again.

"Hey," Stone stepped in. "They're making us leave soon. Can Manny come in and say goodnight?"

"Of course," Kit said as Loni's mouth hung open.

"He's still here?" she asked Kit with wide eyes.

"He wouldn't budge till he knew you were okay, then he stuck around in case he got to see you," Stone said, and that smile widened on Loni's face, warming Kit's heart too.

Stone waved at the door, and Kit watched Manny nervously walk in.

"Hey, Loni," he offered a soft smile. "Sorry, you had such a hard day."

"It's okay; I slept through most of it," she offered.

"Here is your phone," he stepped over and handed it to her. "Lissa gave it to me to give to you."

"Thanks, Manny."

"I added my number in there. You can text me anytime."

"I wake up at weird times here," she warned him.

"Anytime," he said again.

As Kit and Stone were grinning over this cute exchange, Luca had one eye open and smirked; Loni and Manny were unaware.

"What's this about an imaginary date, I hear?" Luca's sudden voice seemed to echo through the room, and Kit had to bite back a laugh when Manny jumped. Stone, on the other hand, cracked up.

"It was... um," Manny scratched his head.

"Dad, it was imaginary," Loni huffed.

"It was just for fun, really. I'd ask before taking her on a real date," Manny assured Luca.

"Plus, he tried to imaginary meet you and get your approval, but I didn't let him," Loni added.

Stone started laughing harder, but Kit gave him a look to shut it.

"That is adorable," Kit cooed, and Manny blushed.

"Mom," Loni shot her a mortified look.

"Sorry, I didn't mean to gush," Kit said sheepishly.

"Least she didn't say it was smooth," Luca teased.

"You're such an ease dropper, dad," Loni made a face. "Anyway, you can't honestly be opposed to imaginary dates?"

"I'm not. You two can have pretend dates," Luca agreed.

"And real ones when I leave this place," Loni pressed.

"At Leo's," Luca agreed.

"Dad," she whined.

"I'm kidding; you can have real dates," Luca glanced at Manny, and the kid relaxed. "I trust ya, kid.

"Thanks, Luca, that means a lot."

"Really! Thanks, dad," Loni was lighting up, and Luca was smiling fondly at her face, as was Kit.

Something to hope for and look forward to outside of this hospital was exactly what Loni needed.

After lights out, Kit found herself lying awake in the on-call room bed next to Luca, who was, for once, sleeping well. Kit knew she needed sleep too, but Luca needed it desperately... he'd been shouldering all their breakdowns throughout this whole thing. That's who he was to Kit and their girls. Luca was their knight, safe space, and protector, but this was killing him too.

Kit's mind couldn't and wouldn't stop; she found herself analyzing everything the doctors said, trying to read between the lines. One of the interns had asked for her both her dad and mother's information earlier. Apparently, they couldn't find Kit's birth records as the hospital she was born at no longer existed. It didn't make sense to need her parent's information since it was apparent the heart condition came from Luca's mom. Unless they thought Loni might need surgery and wanted as much relatives' information as possible in the case, they needed blood donors.

That was Kit's biggest fear. Would Loni need to have her chest opened and her heart repaired? From what she'd read on her phone, it was more than possible that was what was next. Why else would they be calling the best cardiologist in the country?

Needing to move and clear her head, Kit got up and left the room. The bright white lights were off, leaving the dull emergency lights in their place. It was so quiet this late at night, almost peaceful, which felt like a weird way to describe a hospital. It was empty besides a doctor sitting in a chair outside Loni's door. Was that Dr. Blake? As she drew a little close, she saw it was.

"Jenny, you have to stop calling," An urgent whisper filled the quiet space. "I'm on duty tonight. I can't..."

"Yes, she's asleep, but it doesn't matter. I need to be diligent in case she needs me."

"I am not making excuses not to talk about this," he muttered.

"I got to go. I'll call you when I'm off shift."

Kit stepped forward, and he cringed as he noticed her.

"I'm so sorry. I only answered because she kept calling. I promise I was just in to check on Loni. She's asleep and doing fine."

"It's okay," Kit sat in the chair across from him. "It was a five-second call."

"Thanks, Mrs. Donato." He looked relieved. "I've been trying to stay in contact with my dad. That's why I have my cell on."

"You can just call me Kit and my husband, Luca," Kit said with a shrug.

"All right, Kit, again, I'm sorry for coming off unprofessional."

"Don't worry about it, girlfriend trouble?"

"Yeah," he sighed.

"She's not... the, her; I look like, is she?" Kit tilted her head curiously. "Sorry to blurt it out, it's been nagging at me, and Luca noticed you staring too. Careful, he can get protective."

"No... oh crap? You thought I thought you looked like a girlfriend or something. No... it's not like that at all," he shuddered.

"Hey! I may be a mom to teenagers, but it's not like I'm some old hag or something!"

"I just keep making this worse," Dr. Blake groaned. "It's because you look like my sister."

"Oh, okay, I don't feel so bad about the shudder now," Kit laughed. "Really?"

"Yeah, like a lot like her," he studied her momentarily. "It freaked me out a little at first, but I'm getting used to it."

"That's odd," Kit mentioned. "You have a picture of her? I want to see."

"Uh, no, not on this phone." A cloud crossed his face, and she got a strong feeling he didn't want to talk about his sister.

"So, what's going on with the girlfriend?" she asked instead.

"I couldn't. That would be so inappropriate," Dr. Blake hesitated. "Besides, you have enough on your mind."

"I'd love a distraction, actually. I'm good at advice; I used to help my cousin Jase all the time, whether he wanted it or not."

Dr. Blake laughed. "Okay, it wouldn't hurt to get an outside perspective."

"Yes," she urged him on.

"My girlfriend, Jenny, and I are at a crossroads. I don't know what to do. I am in the part of my career where I will always be working. I will have overnights and shifts that sometimes drag on for days. I will be called away in the middle of the night, and so on. She... hates it."

Kit took a moment to digest his words. "I can understand that being hard for her, saying it out loud, don't you?"

"Yes, I do," Dr. Blake said earnestly. "But I told her at the start that this was my lifelong dream and it would be tough. She said she would be around for the ride, and we'd get through it. But now it's always a problem; whenever I can't go to something, miss something, or work late, she gets mad, and we fight."

"How long have you been together?" Kit asked.

"Two years. I was in med school and interning and just as busy as now, if not more at the start, but it wasn't an issue back then." He added with a bitter tone to his voice.

"People's needs can change, especially when you're young and figuring out life," Kit offered. "What are her dreams? Was she as career-minded as you and changed?"

"No, she went to school for business management, and she has a job at a bank, a normal Monday through Friday job. She's never really talked about any major career goals, but she mentions wanting to be a mom sometimes."

"Have you and her talked about kids, like the two of you having them?"

He paled and shook his head, "no, I'm so busy right now. How could I even manage kids?"

"I?" Kit questioned.

"I mean we." He quickly corrected.

"Have you discussed the future with her at all?"

"It's one of the things I avoid," he admitted with a sheepish look.

"Why?"

"I don't know. I guess, I don't know what it looks like yet outside of the hospital goals."

"Has she come to you wanting to talk about the future?"

"No, lately she only comes to me to yell at me," he quipped, and Kit laughed.

"Can I be blunt?"

"Yeah, go for it."

"It's not going to work out with you two."

"Wow, okay, that was blunt."

"You're a doctor. You deal in facts," Kit said, and Dr. Blake cracked a slight smile at that. "You and Jenny are not only on different pages, but I think subconsciously, you both know it's not going to work out, which is why you've avoided discussing a future."

"Or we're young, and we haven't had time."

"You said yourself you're at a crossroads," she reminded him. "Look, there's love, and there's end-game love. End-game love finds a way; even if it has to risk a career or be willing to sacrifice, it finds a way, and nothing stops it. But you and Jenny aren't finding a way; you're just having the same fight over and over. It's not either of your faults; you just don't align."

"Huh." He sat back with a dumbfounded look on his face.

"Was that way too much? I'm sorry!"

"No, it was helpful," he mumbled. "I think you made some good points. It's complicated. When we met, I was in a bad place, and she pulled me out of it."

"That can make it a lot harder to let go, I'd imagine," Kit offered.

"Yeah, but hanging on like this, we're both miserable."

"Not healthy for either of you," Kit said. "Take some time, think about it."

"I will. Thanks for that, really."

"Mom? Dad?" Loni's hoarse voice called out.

"Right here, Loni!" Kit followed Dr. Blake into Loni's room. She was waking up and looking confused and slightly bewildered, but her eyes relaxed as they landed on Kit, who hurried over to sit at her bedside while Dr. Blake took her vitals.

"Your heart rate is a little high; let's take deep breaths, in and out." Dr. Blake coached Loni.

Loni took some slow breaths in and out as Dr. Blake watched the machines closely, and Kit held her hand; it seemed to take several minutes before he was happy with whatever the machine said.

"That's better," Dr. Blake said in a kind and calming tone as he spoke to Loni. "Did you feel scared when you woke up?"

"A little," Loni agreed. "I don't know why it's like this panicky feeling all of a sudden."

Dr. Blake nodded, a flicker of concern in his eyes. "I think you should stay in here, Kit. So, she stays calm."

"Of course," Kit breathed a sigh of relief, and Loni was already moving over to make room for her. Kit came and lay beside her, putting an arm around her daughter and pulling her close.

"I'll be right outside, and I'll let Luca know where you are when he wakes up," Dr Blake offered as he stepped towards the door.

"Thanks, Dr. Blake," Kit said.

"You know what? It will be so confusing when my dad gets here; you can just call me Gus." Dr. Blake offered before he ducked out of the room.

"Gus?" Kit breathed the name out into the air.

"Mom. You, okay?" Loni was peering at her. "You just got all pale."

"It's silly, honey; Gus is my brother's name. It threw me for a loop to hear it, I guess."

"Your brother?" Loni furrowed her eyebrows in confusion. "I didn't know you had a brother."

"It's hard to explain, but technically, I don't. My mother never wanted me to know them, and I never did; all I ever knew were their names."

"But why?"

"She had her reasons, just like she had her reasons for leaving me. I don't think I'll ever understand them," Kit said with a sad sigh as Loni rested her head on her shoulder.

"I'm sorry, mom."

"Don't be, sweetheart. I love your dad, you, and your sister with my whole soul, and that love healed any old wounds I had. You just get some rest, okay?"

Kit stroked her hair as Loni lay against her, and slowly the teenager drifted back to sleep.

Kit's mind was turning as she lay there; she saw an image of Gus's haunted eyes when she first saw him... "You look just like her."

His sister.

Why would she look just like his sister unless...

Could it be? Was Gus Blake the same Gus as her brother?

No. No way, that would be impossible, right?

Chapter 11

Stone pulled up to the house, and Manny stepped out of the car first. He followed the sullen kid inside. Hopefully, Luca's surprise had arrived already, which might lift the kid's spirits. The music shop said they'd deliver it today.

Ava looked up from the table as they walked in. "You're back early?"

"Loni wasn't feeling well enough for visitors today," Stone explained, her face filled with understanding.

"I'm sorry," she said softly as she stepped closer to Manny. "Rest is important for her, though."

"I'm not mad I couldn't see her. I'm worried. They say she's not feeling well; what does that even mean? Why are they just watching her get worse? Why aren't they fixing her goddamn heart!"

"Manny!" Ava exclaimed as she raised a hand to her heart.

"I didn't mean it. I'm sorry I said that," Manny muttered.

"You are understandably upset and worried, but Loni needs us to keep our faith now more than ever. She needs our prayers, not our anger."

He faltered at that, and his lip quivered as he nodded.

"Loni would appreciate how much you care, Kiddo," Stone offered.

"I haven't known her that long. But it doesn't take long to see how special Loni is. When I walked into Leo's to apply, I was so nervous. Luca was sitting at a table, looking so intimidating. The restaurant was so big and beautiful, and I thought I couldn't work at a nice place like that. I almost turned and left."

He paused for a moment as a wistful smile crossed his face. "Then Loni comes out of the kitchen, and, wow. She was so pretty. She looked like she belonged in the movies or something. And she looked at me and smiled, and said, hey come on in, and it wasn't just any smile. I felt welcome in a place I'd never have before. Once I started working there, she always went out of her way to make sure I was good. I heard her telling her dad to be nice to me, and he was too. But not like Loni; no one is as sweet as her."

"I just... I need her to be okay. This isn't fair, mom." Manny's eyes filled with tears, as were Ava's, as she pulled him into her arms. "It's so unfair. Why her?"

"I know it's not fair, Manny. I know," she soothed him. "Somethings don't make sense. Let's go to the church and say some prayers for Loni today. How does that sound?"

He pulled back and wiped at his eyes. "Maybe a little later. I'm going to go lay down for a bit. I need some alone time."

"Okay, we'll go after lunch."

"Wait." Stone stopped him before he walked up the stairs. "You know who you remind me of?"

"Who?"

"My son-in-law," Stone said. "That's how he always spoke about my daughter. With that same conviction and I knew right away that he was family. And now, so are you; you're part of this family. So I don't ever want to hear you saying you don't belong. We got you, okay? And we're all going to make sure Loni pulls through. We have to."

"Thanks, Stone." Manny stood there momentarily and then surprised Stone by throwing his arms around him.

Stone noticed Ava watching with teary eyes as they hugged. When they parted, Manny darted upstairs.

"That was very kind of you," Ava said softly.

"It was true." He entered the kitchen and pulled a box of Easy Mac down.

"Let me make lunch." Ava stopped him. "I picked up a few things today."

"I have the cash I keep in a coffee can in the cabinet for food and stuff. Replace whatever you spent with it, and next time grab money from there." Stone frowned, she couldn't afford to be doing that.

"My son and I are eating the food too." She took some chicken, seasoned it, and placed it in a pan. "It's the least I can do after you bought Manny a guitar."

"It did arrive!" Stone perked up. "Good, that'll cheer Manny up."

"I put it in the closet for now. So you can gift it to him. I shouldn't accept it; you've already done too much."

"It's from Luca, and he told me to tell you it's as much for Loni as it is for Manny."

"How so?" She turned to raise a dubious eyebrow.

"It's been bugging Loni that he had to sell his guitar," Stone explained. "Luca thinks it'll be a big cheer-up for her if he can go in and play it for her."

"Since it's for Loni," she agreed with a smile. "I'd have already said yes anyhow, though. I feel bad about him having to sell it, to begin with. Their creative outlets are so important."

As she spoke, she leaned over to put the chicken in the oven, and Stone quickly averted her eyes from her shapely butt. She was slightly older than Kit and Luca but was probably ten years younger than Stone. He had no business checking her out, and he knew it.

"If it makes you feel better, my daughter, at one point, was putting every scrap of extra money into savings to send my nephew Jase to college." Stone offered. "I had custody of him after his folks died."

"Because you couldn't afford to?" Ava asked as she put a pot of water on the stove.

"No, I screwed up and lost his inheritance money at the casino."

"Oh!" Her eyes widened at that.

"I was not a great parent, but Kit and I still had a tight bond. It was just her and I, until we moved here for Jase."

"I understand that. Manny and I have been alone since before he was born," Ava said. "His dad took off when I was still pregnant."

"Asshole," Stone muttered. "Stacey waited until Kit was two. I wake up one day, and she's gone; all she left was a note."

"My word," Ava sighed sadly. "How does a mother leave their child? I can't fathom it."

"I was angry at her for a long time, but eventually, I had to brush it off and keep going. Kit needed me."

"Well, good for you raising a daughter all by yourself," Ava said, not a hint of sarcasm, just genuine honesty in her tone. "It's not always easy, but when it's just the two of you, you do form a special bond. You are a good dad, Stone. A little unconventional, but a good one."

"Thanks. My point wasn't for you to make me feel better, though."

"Well at least you had a roof over her head."

"Ava, don't do that. There are bad parents out there who make bad decisions. You aren't one of them. You were doing everything possible, and Manny was trying to help."

"Thank you for that."

"What is that!?" Stone asked as she dumped some black stuff into the pot of water on the stove.

"Rice."

"Why is it black?"

"Because it's wild rice, it's better for you."

She then pulled a big head of broccoli from the fridge.

"What is that now!?"

"Don't tell me you're never seen broccoli? It's called a vegetable," Ava said in a mocking tone. "It's in the cabbage family. It's full of vitamins and-"

"I know what it is. Why is it on my counter instead of Mac and cheese? Or mashed potatoes or something good."

"It's green, you should like it," Ava teased.

"I'm not eating that crap."

"Stone." She turned and gave him a stern look. "Your daughter is going through a nightmare. She can't have you getting sick too. It's time to start taking care of yourself better."

"You're shaming me again!"

"Call it what you want; you know I'm right," she quipped. "A few vegetables aren't going to hurt you."

"Fine, but I'm not giving up weed," he sulked.

"I wouldn't dare ask that." A smirk tugged at her lips. "Although you could consider switching to edibles."

He looked up with a thunderous look, and she held her hands up in surrender.

"Okay, one battle at a time."

"Lissa, what are you doing? Loni asked as Lissa pulled her socks off.

"I'm panting your toenails."

"Why?" Loni whined irritably. "My feet are all swollen and gross; leave them alone."

"Because they can be swollen and gross and still have pretty nails," Lissa declared. "It might make you feel better."

"I doubt toenail polish is going to make me feel better."

Loni had woken up feeling awful. She'd been sweating all night and was dehydrated with a terrible headache. Her chest felt heavy, like when you had a chest cold, but different, worse. Then as the day went on, she kept getting small pulses of pain, almost like cramps in her chest near her heart. Dr. Morgan was extremely concerned about it. Doctors had been in and out all day. They had just taken her in for more chest X-rays and were studying them next door.

All this was taking a toll on Loni that panicky feeling she woke up with never went away and it was making her feel so crabby. She was glad they sent Manny and Andrea home, she'd not be good company today, she'd been snapping at Lissa all morning.

"Oh, I don't know about that," Gus had just walked in. "My sister always said a little color goes a long way."

"Yes! That!" Lissa agreed eagerly. "Which one, blue or pink?"

"Pink," Loni and Gus said at the same time.

"I knew she'd say that," Lissa said gleefully as she got started.

"What did Dr. Morgan say about the scans? Is she talking to my parents?"

"No, she sent them to the cafeteria to get lunch. She's going over them with my dad on the phone now." Gus came over to check the machines as he spoke. "He got on a direct plane last night. He should be here today, soon, hopefully."

"Their bad then?" Loni guessed.

"I didn't see them, Loni," Gus said softly. "Just keep your-"

"Yeah, yeah, keep my spirits up," Loni sighed.

"On the plus side, that's a fabulous shade of pink," Gus offered to make Lissa giggle, and Loni smiled slightly.

"Her feet are still so swollen," Luca's voice was full of worry as he and Kit walked in.

"Oh, uh, Gus hey," Kit looked nervous as she glanced at Gus, and Luca nudged her, but she ignored him.

"I know." Gus was jotting down some stuff from Loni's machines on his clipboard. He set it down and reached for his phone.

"I'm going to make sure my dad has a car ready to pick him up at the airport," Gus said. "I'll be back."

He ducked out of the room quickly. One of the things Loni had observed here was how fast doctors walked, it was seriously impressive.

"Will you just ask him and quit being all weird," Luca said as he glanced at Kit.

"Ask him what?" Lissa asked as she carefully held Loni's foot while applying the nail polish.

"Luca, stop," Kit groaned. "What am I supposed to do, corner him and say, is Stacey Woods your mom?"

"Well yeah.." Luca said as Gus suddenly walked back in.

"Forgot my clipboard," Gus explained as he went to grab it.

"Who is Stacey Woods?" Lissa asked.

"What?" Gus froze and looked at her with questioning eyes. "How do you know my mom's name?"

"Ding ding!" Luca exclaimed, to which Kit glared at him.

"What is going on?" Loni asked curiously.

"Congratulations, you just got an uncle," Luca quipped.

"What!?" Gus and the two girls all asked at the same time.

"Luca, seriously." Kit shot him a dark look and then looked at Gus. "Ignore my husband. His humor has terrible timing."

"What is going on, Kit?" Gus's eyes flashed with the same confusion Loni was feeling.

"Stacey Woods is my mother too," Kit said, causing, Loni and Gus's jaws to drop.

"What?" Gus breathed out in a stunned tone. "I don't understand. How?"

"Dr. Blake is our uncle?" Lissa questioned as she put the top back on the nail polish. "How, come we never met him or your mom then?"

"Because she left her as a baby," Loni explained.

"No. My mom wouldn't do that." Gus was shaking his head.

"I know this is confusing." Kit looked at Lissa for a moment and then back at Gus. "It all came to me when you said your name. The one time I spoke with her, her two kids were in the background, and-"

"Stacey Woods is not an uncommon name," he cut in. "This is probably a mistake."

"Then why do I look just like your sister?" Kit questioned. "You said it yourself. You said eerily so."

"It could be a coincidence," Gus's tone was faltering.

Dr. Morgan burst into the room with several interns and Dr. Gupta, interrupting the tense moment. Her grim face made Loni's gut twist.

"What is it?" Loni asked.

"Lissa, why don't you go outside, hon?" Dr. Morgan suggested.

"I want to hear too!"

"It's fine. Just tell us what's going on." Kit walked over and gave Lissa's shoulder a squeeze as Luca came to clasp Loni's hand.

"The damage to Loni's heart is getting much worse. The left ventricle is showing severe inflammation. We can't allow the damage to get any worse."

"What does that mean?" Luca asked, tightening his grip on Loni's hand.

"We need to repair it," Dr. Morgan said.

"Surgically?" Kit questioned in a frightened whisper.

"You have to do surgery on my heart?" Loni repeated as Luca's grip became tighter. "Dad, loosen up."

"Sorry." He loosened his hold, but his jaw remained tense.

"Yes, we do. Loni, I know you're scared. I've done this procedure many times," Dr. Morgan said gently. "Dr. Blake Senior is on his way and will scrub in with me when he arrives. In addition, Dr. Blake Junior will be right there too."

"Oh god," Kit sobbed.

"Mom?" Lissa whimpered.

"Dr. Blake Junior will keep you two updated throughout this whole thing." Dr. Morgan promised.

"You have put her through heart surgery?" Luca finally spoke, his voice hardly a whisper.

"When?" Loni asked nervously.

"Right now. We can't waste any time."

"Why are we in here? Why did they tell us not to bring Lissa? It's bad. That means it's bad." Luca was firing off questions as he paced Dr. Morgan's office.

Kit meanwhile sat at the extended meeting table, wringing her hands. It had been eight hours since their little girl had been wheeled off to surgery. Finally, Gus, the brother she was still trying to wrap her head around, came and said Loni made it through surgery, but he looked grim. He told them to wait in here. Lissa was passed out, and he suggested they leave her to sleep and talk to her later. In Gus's opinion, whatever they were about to tell them was too much for Lissa to hear. That was terrifying them both.

Finally, Gus came back into the room with two interns.

"What's going on? What's happening?" A panicked Kit asked.

"My dad will be in soon to talk to you." Gus sat in front of Kit. "But I haven't told him yet—"

Dr. Morgan and a tall, dark-haired man in blue scrubs walked in. Luca immediately stood up and walked over to them.

"What's happening!? Talk to us, please."

"Mr. Donato, I assume?" The doctor Kit assumed was Gus's dad Dr. Johnathan Blake responded.

"Call me Luca, please tell us what's going on with Loni?"

"I suggest sitting down, Luca," he said calmly.

Why? Why would he tell him that?

"I'm not doing anything until you tell me what's going on!"

Kit found herself speechless, her heart racing as her stomach knitted with worry.

"I was able to repair the damage to her left ventricle... for now."

"What does that mean, for now?"

"The Brugada syndrome is aggressively attacking Loni's heart, and it's going to continue to do so. I can't control the condition with her heart as damaged as it is. Which means that what I did will only buy her time, and we'll be right back here, again. Each time worse then the last."

He paused, and Kit took in Gus's face, his eyes... they looked so lost. Why? What did that mean?

"So what now, what's next?" Luca asked.

"First, Dr. Morgan will get her on the national donor list."

"What?" Luca gasped as Kit felt a sob escapes her throat.

"I'm sorry to say this bluntly, but time is limited," Dr. Blake continued, his eyes set on Luca as he spoke. "Loni's heart is failing fast, within a month her organs will start shutting down, if not sooner. Not to mention the multitude of other things she's at risk for, including cardiac arrest. We have to act now."

"Okay, okay, than act," Luca cried out. "What do we do? How do we get her a heart?"

"Unforntently, It could take years to get a viable heart. In the meanwhile, there's something we can do to buy her time A surgery we call a hail Mary, because it's often used to buy patients time while on the heart transplant list."

Hail Mary, heart transplant... Kit was stunned silent her eyes darting from one person to the next.

"Dad.." Kit noticed Gus's eyes were wet with tears as he stood up.

"Just a moment, Gus," Dr. Blake looked annoyed to be interrupted.

"But—"

"This is a procedure in which we'd transplant what's called an LVAD into Loni's heart. It's essentially a device that would assist her left ventricle in pumping blood to her heart. We'd still have to monitor her often. But it would—"

"Dad, stop!"

"Gus, what in the world?"

"We don't need it," Gus said. "The Hail Mary surgery. We don't need it."

"Son, I know what I'm doing; this isn't the time to question me."

"Heart transplant? My baby needs a heart transplant!?" Kit finally found words, and they left her throat as a sob.

"Oh, Cricket!" Luca turned and raced over to her, gathering her in his arms "I got you, baby," she collapsed into his arms as he held her tight.

Meanwhile the older Dr. Blake gasped loudly. Kit looked up to find his stunned dark eyes on her face.

"Cricket?" Dr. Blake breathed out. "It can't be.. "

"Dad, that's what I was trying to tell you," Gus said, but his dad hadn't taken his eyes off Kit.

"The resemblance," a stunned Dr. Blake muttered.

"Kit and Gus are brother and sister, and Kit looks just like his sister. We got all that already. Can we get on with what we need to do for Loni? This surgery, when are we doing this? How soon? Please talk to us!" Luca begged as he held Kit tightly in his arms.

"We don't need the Hail Mary," Dr. Blake repeated Gus's earlier words as his eyes filled with sadness.

"What? But you said—"

"We don't need it, because there is already a heart for Loni," Gus explained.

"What where?" Kit asked.

"It'll be easier to show you." Gus rose to his feet and so did Dr. Johnathan Blake.

"Let's go."

Chapter 12

"And maybe then you'll hear the words I been singing. Funny how when you're dead, people start listening."

The wind picked up, and the mother hugged her arms around herself.

"It's getting late," she mumbled into the air.

Her gaze fell to the two red rose bushes that made their return this year. London would be so thrilled! Maybe it would help thaw the icy chill that had set over their relationship during the last year.

Sweet sixteen, they say? The mother smiled as she thought, one could hope. Year fifteen was challenging, to say the least.

Nonetheless, her daughter had promised she would come today. "I wouldn't miss it, mom. It's our day. Every year, no matter what is going on."

"Where are you, London?"

The mother began to pace through the field of flowers. The sun would go down soon; why wasn't she here yet?

An uneasy feeling came over the mother as she waited for that little red car to pull up. An early birthday present, as London had gotten her license a week early. She'd fought her about the art school and hoped the car would be an olive branch.

A noise in the distance nicked at her brain, but she ignored it as she continued to pace.

"London!?" Her voice was starting to take on a panicked tone.

"Where are you!?"

"I'm here, mama. I'm right here."

She whirled around to face her beautiful daughter, her long red hair whipping in the wind, as was her long white dress.

"London—"

"It's time, mom, don't be sad," London's voice was so soft, so beautiful.

"What do you mean? Time for what?"

"Mom, I don't need you anymore, but they do."

She ignored that and the noise.. she started hearing it again, a pounding noise. Where was it coming from?

"Look, sweetheart, the roses are back," the mother said instead. "Come sit with me."

"It's time to let me go."

"No..."

London faded from her eyes as the pounding grew louder, and soon the entire flower field began to disappear too.

"No!" She sobbed.

The field, the flowers, were all gone, and as the mother's eyes adjusted to the same old white room she'd spent most of the last six years in. Her gaze first landed on the walls, full of all the flowers London had sketched over the years.

"Stacey! Open up. Your son is here for you!" Came a voice from behind the door, but she ignored it.

Stacey looked down from the bed she was perched on, it was always a shock to come out of her dreams and face reality. Her eyes filled with tears as she took in London lying there, those honey brown eyes closed to the world, that sweet face that blushed so easily pale and unresponsive.

"I can't, sweetheart. I can't let you go."

Kit stood outside a hospital door, confused and worried, as a nurse knocked inessentially on a door. Why was it locked anyway? Neither Gus nor his dad had bothered to explain anything but said she needed to come along.

They were at a care facility about a half hour from the hospital. Being away from Loni right now was killing her. Gus's dad, who insisted that Kit call him John, had assured her that Loni wouldn't wake up for some time yet. Still though, every moment away from her daughter added to her unease.

Unfortunately, this also meant Luca wasn't there with Kit, as he had to be with Loni. From the sounds of the name, Stacey, being called as the nurse knocked on the door. It appeared Kit was about to come face to face with the woman who abandoned her, without her husband to get her through it. She took a brave breath, this was about Loni, for some reason she didn't get, but she would do anything for her girl right now.

Finally, the door was opened, and Gus and John walked in first. Kit stood behind them, being as petite as she was; Stacey hadn't noticed her yet. Kit, however, could look at her mother for the first time. Well, the first time that she could remember, anyhow.

Stacey was a few years younger than her dad and yet she looked so old. Her face was heavily weathered with wrinkles. Her hair had gone stark white, and her soft brown eyes were murky and tired looking. How did she look this terrible?

As Kit's gaze moved from her mother to the bed beyond her, the reason for Stacey's state made itself known.

On the bed behind Stacey, a young redhead woman was hooked up to machines.

"That's her? that's London?" Kit asked as she stepped forward. "My sister?"

As Kit drew closer, she was stunned. London looked so much like her; it was like looking in a mirror, well a mirror ten or so years ago, but still. It was shocking.

Stacey gasped and clasped a hand over her heart. "Cricket.. I how?"

Her eyes moved from Kit to Gus and then to John.

"What is this? Why are the three of you together? What is the meaning of this?" Stacey demanded. "Johnathan, you told him?"

Thirty four years and Stacey looked at her for all of five seconds, it didn't surprise Kit much

"You knew about her?" Gus asked his dad with a stunned expression.

"I.. found out. It— it doesn't matter now, son."

"It's why he left me," Stacey said bluntly. "He promised he'd never tell you. Please, Gus. Don't. Don't think less of me than you already do."

"Stacey, we don't have time to make you feel better right now," John's voice was clipped. His eyes fell on London and filled with sadness. "Cricket needs your help. Her child is sick, but we can help her."

"What?" Stacey's eyes softened as she finally looked at Kit again. "Your baby girl? I saw her on Facebook just once; I—She's sick?"

Kit's stomach was knotted up. She'd spent her entire life angry and hurt over this woman. Once she had children those wounds finally healed and she let it all go. Now she found herself feeling so sad for Stacey, it was overshadowing the bitterness.

"She's very sick," John confirmed. "And she's not a baby anymore; she's sixteen."

"London was sixteen..." Stacey's voice trembled as tears dripped from her eyes.

"What happened to her?" Kit asked softly.

"A car accident." John looked haunted as he glanced at the bed.

"Is she.. will she ever be ok?"

"No," Gus breathed the word out.

"She could be! Someday! Don't say that!" Stacey looked at him with horror in her eyes.

"You have to stop living in denial, Stacey. She's brain dead." The pain in John's eyes went straight to Kit's heart.

"Oh god.." Kit started to realize what that meant and why they were there.

"But her heart is fine," Gus added as he looked at Kit. "My sister... our sister, can save your daughter."

"The heart for Loni, is London's heart?" Kit dropped to her knees, a sob leaving her throat.

No.. no, how cruel was that? It couldn't be.

"What? Her heart?" Stacey whispered in a horrified gasp.

"Stacey, Loni's heart is failing and she needs a transplant. London and Loni have the same blood type and are closely related. That along with them being close to the same size, makes her the most viable donor we could ever ask for." John spoke up as he wiped a tear from the corner of his eye.

"No!" Stacey shrieked. "Are you insane!? She could wake up!"

"You know she can't. The longer she stays like this the less chance she can help anyone. Over time her organs will become less viable—"

"No, I can't." She cut him off. "I won't let you cut her up. I won't let you take her away!"

"Stacey, please! It's unfair to hold on to her like this. I've let this go all this time. I didn't want to fight you on it, but now.. your grandchild's life is at stake here."

"No!" Stacey whipped past him and ran from the room, and he ran after her.

Gus took Kit's arm and helped her to her feet. It wasn't like having Luca but it was comforting.

"We'll talk her into it; we have to," Gus promised as they parted. Her heart swelled with affection and empathy for him, just starting out in life and he loses his sister? If only she could have been there for him.

"I... I get it," Kit walked over to her sister. "If this was Loni or Lissa, I don't know if could do it either."

"It's been six years; she's never going to wake up," Gus said. "She's only alive because of these machines."

"Hey London, I'm your sister, Cricket, but everyone calls me Kit. Your- er our mom sucked at names back then, but yours is beautiful." Kit rested a hand against her cheek. It was so cold and dry. "This is so unfair. You were just a baby."

Kit looked at all the drawings of all the flowers on the walls. "You draw too? So does my girl, Loni, your niece. I always wondered where she got it from. Now I know."

"I wish I'd have gotten to know you," Kit added. "You deserved to have your big sister in your life. You and Gus both did, but don't blame your mom, okay? I blamed her enough for all of us, and I can't be angry at her anymore. Not now. No mama should ever have to say goodbye to their baby."

"I still can't believe my mom had a family before us," Gus mumbled.

"They never married, my dad and Stacey. She said she was young, overwhelmed, drinking all the time. She said she left for me," Kit explained. "Said I was safer without her there."

"Then why didn't she ever come back?"

"I got her number from my dad and called her once. I asked her her that. She said she didn't want to disrupt you and London's lives. You were ten at the time and she was only six."

"We would've loved to know you.. I don't get that." Gus frowned.

"I think she was afraid of losing your respect. Not just you two, at that point your dad didn't know either. Can you imagine finding out your spouse had a child that they left behind?"

"No. I guess I see why he left her, he never told us. I chose to live with my dad after the divorce. Mom and I never got along great after that. London stayed with her, and they were always so close, until that last year."

"This is— I can't." Kit looked at Gus with a sigh. "I can't take her heart." .

"You have to," Gus said in a trembling voice. "It could be years when and if we ever find another viable donor for Loni. Even if we do, the chances of anyone matching as good as London is slim. That's and I hate saying this, but that's if she makes it it that long."

Kit looked at him sharply. "Your dad said that other surgery could buy her years."

"It could, if everything goes right, but she'll still have a heart condition, and she'll still have flare ups, infections and all kind of things. Any of those complications could kill her. I know this is blunt but, it's true. If there is a viable heart for a heart patient. Time is so important."

"But Stacey, she won't—"

"She will," Gus said determinedly. "She's been living in denial for so long. But she can't now, not anymore. I was so angry at her for keeping our sister tied to this bed. London deserved to be able to pass on and find peace. At least now, it was for a reason."

"But if there is any chance she could recover.."

"There isn't."

Kit choked back another sob. "So you're telling me the only way to save Loni is to convince the woman who left me to pull the plug on her baby girl?"

"It's not the only way." John stepped back inside.

"What do you mean? Where's Stacey?"

"I couldn't find her; she ran off," he sighed. "If I have to get a court order, I will. As London's father, I have rights here too."

"I don't think you'll have to," Gus said. "She won't let her granddaughter suffer when she can help her."

"I hope you're right.. but Stacey doesn't care about me like she does you and your sister. She never wanted me to know me even when I was an adult."

"It wasn't because she didn't care," John said. "She didn't think she deserved to know you. She was ashamed. When I found her looking at your Facebook pictures, she was sobbing and heartbroken. Every year on London's birthday, she would get so depressed. Once I found out about you, she explained it was because of the resemblance. She saw London get older every year and never got to see you grow up too."

"I don't know what to think..."

"She was always so overly attached to London. Overprotective and paranoid that she'd lose her someday," Gus noted. "It was weird, she wasn't like that with me."

"And then she did lose her," Kit shuddered as she looked down at her comatose sister.

"She blames herself. She bought London the car she crashed in." John informed her.

"That doesn't make it her fault!" Kit's heart ached for the very woman who had broken her as a child.

"It wasn't just the car," Gus added. "London wanted to go away to art school, and mom said no. They spent nearly a whole year fighting about it. The car was like mom's bribe to get her back, and then she crashed it, on the way to the damn flower field they met at every year."

"No," Kit shook her head sadly. How does a mother recover from that?

"I feel awful for her I honestly do. It's the biggest reason I haven't pursued legal action yet to get Stacey to let London go," John admitted. "But, I think some part of me didn't want to let her go either."

"I understand. I don't think I could either," Kit empathized.

John walked up to the bed and rested a hand against London's pale cheek as a tear slid down his face. "But that isn't fair. It's selfish to keep you here, Little Red. You deserve to fly with the angels."

Kit found herself crying at that, as was Gus. She never thought she'd meet her siblings but always longed to. She never thought if she did, it would be like this.

"Couldn't we do the Hail Mary surgery for now? Give Stacey more time to accept this. Maybe if she met Loni, she'd. I don't know." Kit suggested tiredly.

"If we can avoid that surgery, we should," John explained. "She's weak; every time she goes under the knife, it's a risk."

"So what do we do?"

"We give Stacey a day, maybe a few, to come to the right decision," John said. "Loni needs time to recover from todays surgery anyhow."

"And if she doesn't?" Gus asked.

"Then I meant what I said. I'll get a court order."

Kit's phone buzzed, indicating a text had come in. It seemed so loud in the quiet room that all three jumped at the noise.

"It's Luca," Kit said as she looked at it. "Lissa is up and asking about Loni, but Loni is still out. What do we tell Lissa? This is going to freak her out so bad!"

"I'll help you talk to her. Let's go," Gus spoke as he hurried out the door, and John was right behind him.

Kit stood for one more moment, looking down at her sister. She thought about her daughters and how close they were. All the sweet memories the two of them had.

She felt so robbed of that with her own sister. She didn't even know London, and yet she loved her.

"Sibling love is pretty special I guess. I know you reached out to Loni before. These purple flowers on the walls, Loni had a dream about them. That was you, right? If you're with her in your own way, watching out for her, thank you."

Kit took a step back, wiping her eyes dry.

"If we do get your heart, I promise we will cherish it with everything. It'll go to a wonderful girl who will do amazing things in her life. She'll carry you with her proudly."

With that, Kit hurried out of the room. In her haste, she didn't notice a teary-eyed Stacey quickly duck out of view as she left the room.

Chapter 13

"Where is Mom? What's going on? Why can't you talk to me? When is Loni going to wake up?"

Lissa fired off one question after another as Luca sat as impatiently as she felt. They were waiting for Kit to get back with the two Blakes. Dr. Morgan was currently with Loni and a few other doctors, watching her closely as she came out of anesthesia. Dr. Morgan had been here since early this morning. Luca was impressed with her dedication to his daughter. He knew she had other patients too, and had seen them coming and going, but Loni seemed to be the only one admitted at the moment.

"Why don't you get candy or something from the vending machine?" Luca suggested.

"I don't want any candy. I want my sister to wake up and be okay. That's all I want."

"I know, Shorty." Luca squeezed her shoulder. "So do I."

"Tell me what's going on, Dad, please," Lissa begged.

The elevator chimed, and Luca was relieved to see Kit and the Blakes emerge. The older Blake nodded at them and then rushed into Loni's room.

"Mom!" Lissa jumped up and nearly lunged toward Kit.

Luca grew concerned at his wife's puffy eyes and tear-stained cheeks. They'd both been crying nonstop, but what could've made her break down badly when she left? They said they had a heart for Loni right?

"Come here, Lissa," Kit took Lissa in her arms, closing her eyes and smelling her hair as she embraced her.

"What's going on, baby?" Luca asked, and Kit looked up at him.

"Let's all sit down," Gus suggested.

Kit had Lissa's hand in hers as they made their way to the chairs.

"Uncle Gus what's going on? I know you all think I'm a kid but I need to know," Lissa demanded.

Gus looked taken aback, but the corners of his lips twisted into a slight smile.

"Uncle," he murmured. "Never thought I'd be able to hear someone call me that."

"Was that weird? Should I not have?" Lissa asked.

"I don't mind at all. That's what I am." He ruffled her hair and a sad look flickered in his eyes as he did.

"So what's wrong with Loni? Why did you have to take my mom somewhere?"

"Lissa, one question at a time," Kit chided gently.

"It's okay, Kit," Gus said. "I get it. It stinks sitting out here and not knowing anything. I'll talk to you about Loni. It's a lot and it might be a little confusing and scary. Just let me know if you have questions, okay?"

"Okay." Lissa nodded, her eyes were full of worry as she focused on Gus. Kit sniffled beside him, and Luca put his arm around her as she let Gus take the lead.

"Remember I told you before that what was happening was pretty serious?"

"Yeah," Lissa said softly. "You said you knew how I felt. You were there on the worst night of your parent's life. What did that mean?"

Gus exchanged a look with Kit and then met Lissa's gaze again. "I'll get to that. For starters, let's talk about Loni. You understand she has a heart condition, right?"

"Yes, the same thing my grandma Elizabeth had."

"Right, it's called Brugada syndrome. It was dormant in Loni until sometime recently. We suspect it started showing symptoms a month or so ago. The rapid heart rate it can cause can lead to many things, including heart attacks. The damage to Loni's heart indicates she had one."

"Loni had a heart attack!?"

"Likely a very mild one in her sleep," Gus continued in a calm voice. Lissa surprised Luca by quieting down and continuing to listen intently.

"But even though it was mild, it still caused damage to her heart. Since she didn't know, the damage got worse as it festered," Gus continued. "Meanwhile, her heart condition continued to act up. That started to aggravate that damage further. The problem here is we can't treat her heart condition with her heart as it is. So what this all means is Loni's heart is too badly damaged to fix—"

"So she is going to die? No, please!" Lissa cried out.

"No," Luca stifled a sob as he reached for Lissa's hand.

"No, hon. We're not going to let her die," Kit said in a shaky voice.

"But.. her heart—"

"Your sister needs a heart replacement," Gus explained quickly. "With Loni's young age, a heart from a viable donor should allow her to live a full life. She'll have to take medication and be on a strict diet. She'll have a lot of doctor appointments her whole life. I'll be honest, these things are never guaranteed, she could still have issues later in life, but it's her best shot."

"But, the only way she could get someone's heart is if they .. died, right?" Lissa whispered the word, her eyes full of horror.

Gus took a long shaky breath as he nodded slowly. "Right, so, uh. That's where we went. Um—"

"I have a sister," Kit spoke up as Gus stammered over his words, and he looked relieved.

"A sister?" Lissa asked.

"She got into a bad accident when she was Loni's age," Kit explained. "She hurt her head. Very bad, so bad that she can't wake up."

Luca immediately realized what that meant. His heart ached for Kit, for Gus and his dad. He tightened his hold around Kit's shoulder, and she leaned into his touch.

"I have an aunt? But she's hurt?"

"She's more than just hurt, she's called brain dead. She can't wake up like your mom said." Gus's eyes were full of pain as he spoke.

"Not ever?"

"No, not ever," Gus confirmed.

"I'm so sorry, Uncle Gus." Lissa frowned.

"Yeah me too," Luca offered. "That's just awful, man."

"That was the worst night you talked about?" Lissa guessed.

"Yeah, it sure was," Gus said with a faraway look in his eyes. After a moment, he shook his head as if shaking the bad memories away. "But the reason why we're telling you this is that the heart Loni needs, my sister can give it to her. Her heart is fine, and she's a perfect donor for Loni."

Good, god... Luca glanced at Kit, who was pale and wiping at her eyes. She finally met her siblings only to find this out.

"But when they take her heart, she'll die, right?" Lissa asked in a shaky voice; her lip quivered, but she didn't waver as she continued to focus on Gus.

Lissa's maturity in this moment filled Luca with pride, but it didn't stop his gut from twisting into a knot. She wasn't supposed to be handling anything like this. At thirteen, her summer was supposed to be full of annoying her sister and getting into trouble with her friends. He'd give anything for sisterly squabbles and angry parents knocking at his door right now.

"London, that's her name, is already dead, Lissa. The only reason she is alive is the machines keeping her that way," Gus explained. "This is our chance to say goodbye and let her go. It's London's chance to have peace finally. And most importantly, it's Loni's chance at a long life."

"When.. are they going to do it? Can I see my aunt first?"

"There's a little roadblock we need to get through first and Loni needs time to recover from the surgery today. But hopefully, within a few weeks."

Loni's phone rang, and Luca's eyes widened. "Who is calling you this late?"

"It's Ruthie. I'll be right back." Lissa said with a frown as she ducked off to answer it.

"I can't—your dad. I don't know how we thank you for this," Luca stammered.

"No need, but—" Gus stammered.

"My mother didn't agree to it," Kit said hurriedly.

"She was there!?" Luca was stunned.

"Seems like she's always there, sitting with her," Kit said as she drew a shaky breath.

"She is," Gus confirmed. "Every day, all day, she's there."

Damn. Not that Luca didn't get it if it was one of his daughters....he shuddered. That thought was way too close to home right now.

"My mom and my dad disagreed with keeping London on machines. But my mom didn't care. She transferred her to a facility near here when I got the job here. She thought I'd be her ally or something against my dad. I didn't agree with it either though, and resented her for putting me in the middle. In turn, she resented me for not standing by my sister. It's been a sad and complicated mess for six years now."

"Where is she, Stacey?" Luca demanded. "I get it, and I want to empathize with her, but screw that. That woman walked out on Kit when she was only a baby, and now she's not even willing to save her grandchild? I got some words for that woman."

"Luca, don't—"

"Cricket, I have to. I will do whatever I have to do for Loni. If I need to rip my own heart out for her, I will. We are not losing her."

"My dad can get a court order. My mom won't fight that; she'll know she can't."

"How can we do that to her? A court order? I can't imagine," Kit spoke in a hushed tone as she shuddered.

"This is for the better of everyone, my mom included. What she's doing right now it's not living. Not even close. She's tied herself to that bed too."

"It feels so cruel," Kit muttered.

"Cruel would be not helping a girl who has a chance to live to hold on to one that already died," Gus said as he stood. "I'm going to go check in on Loni. She should be waking soon. I'll come to get you all in a bit."

"Talk to me, baby. You saw your mom?" Luca asked after Gus left.

"I can't even begin to comprehend my emotions," Kit stood up and started pacing. "Seeing my mother again was so much, but all I could see was my sister in that bed. She looks so much like me. It was like looking back in time."

"I can't imagine meeting your long sister like that." Luca also stood and clasped her hands in his. She stopped pacing and met his gaze.

"There was a part of me, a tiny part, that was always a little bitter about them," Kit confessed. "I know it's terrible; it was never their fault. But it felt like she chose them over me."

"That's completely understandable," Luca said as he brushed a stray red lock from her face.

"I know, but I feel guilty for any negative feelings now. I feel.. robbed. I should've been able to know London, and now I never will. Yet, I have to take her heart from her. I'm just.. my head is a mess, and so is my heart. I feel so sorry for Stacey. I don't hate her anymore, but I still feel like she did me wrong like she did all of us wrong."

"She did," Luca said. "When you called her, she could've changed everything. She had her chance for redemption, and she refused it. You should be angry. I know I am."

"I know, and I was until I saw her, babe. She's aged so badly that she looks twenty years older than she is. She's broken; London's accident broke her. I only feel pity for her. No matter what she did, she never deserved this."

This was why he loved her so much; Kit was never one to hold a grudge. She was a strong and feisty woman, unafraid to tell anyone what she thought. But she was also empathetic and understanding. She got that people were flawed, and she believed in second chances.

"No one deserves that," Luca agreed with that sentiment. "And I believe she's broken. I know I would be, but this is about Loni. We have to fight for our girl."

"I know," Kit said as she gulped nervously. "I will also do whatever I have to do, but if anyone is going to talk to Stacey, it should be me."

"I hate that you're hurting. That we're all hurting." Luca cupped her face in his hands. "I hate that I can't fix this."

"I know," she whispered. "This isn't something one person can fix. But, Luciano, you are the one getting us through this, especially Loni."

"I'm trying, but sometimes I feel like I could just lose my crap and... I don't know."

"I do know. I feel the same way sometimes," Kit lifted her arms to wrap around his neck. He lowered his to her waist, pulling her towards him. She rested her head against his chest and let out a soft sigh as he comforted her.

"That's the hardest part of being a parent, right?" He mused as he ran his hands up and down her back. "We don't get to flip out."

"But we still do; we all have to break down sometimes. Even you." She tilted her head up and gazed at him knowingly.

He rested his forehead against hers and closed his eyes.

"Is everything okay?" They pulled apart as they heard Lissa coming back.

"No, it's not okay," Kit said as Lissa approached them. "But we can't do anything about that. So we just have to be there for each other."

"Okay, Mom." Lissa agreed in a soft tone as Kit pulled her into their hug.

"Why was Ruthie calling so late?" Luca asked once they parted.

"Lucky is upset, he won't sleep. He's been walking around from door to door and whining. They had to open every door and still he kept wandering."

"He's looking for us," Kit sighed.

"Don't worry; I took care of it. I think. Well, I hope," Lissa offered.

"How?" Luca asked curiously.

"I called Grandpa, and he said Lucky can stay there. He's stayed there before when we went on vacation. I thought that way; he won't look for us so much. I also talked to Manny, who said he'd watch out for Lucky. Having someone new to play with him might help too. Uncle Andre is driving him over there now."

"That was a great idea, thank you," Luca praised.

"Speaking of Manny, think they'd make an exception for him to come to see Loni tonight? Him being there when she wakes up would mean so much to her," Kit suggested.

"I'll text Manny and let him know we're asking about it," Luca agreed as he fished his phone out of his pocket.

Gus stepped back out with Dr. Morgan and his dad.

"She should be waking soon," John informed them. "We want to keep her calm and relaxed tonight, so let's not get into anything with her. We'll talk to her about everything tomorrow."

"Is it okay if she has a friend visit tonight? Just until she falls back asleep?" Luca asked, and Dr. Morgan nodded with a soft smile.

"That's fine; it'll be good for her spirits," Dr. Morgan agreed.

"I agree," John said. "It's common during heart failure to feel anxious, on edge, and even get a sense of doom. We want to do everything we can to counteract this. We don't want her falling into a depressive state."

"We won't let that happen," Luca said as he texted Stone and Manny.

It was a relief that there was at least something he could do for her. Even if that something was letting her have a boyfriend, he couldn't deny how Loni lit up whenever Manny was around.

Loni felt as if she'd been asleep for weeks when she finally started to wake she felt numb and her chest felt very heavy like she was underwater.

"She's awake," she heard her mom say.

Someone squeezed her hand. "Hey, Loni."

"Manny?" As she opened her eyes, he slowly came into focus. He sat in a chair at her bedside and held her hand gently in his. "You're here; they let you come?"

"Well, I had to bribe some nurses," he quipped, flashing that winning smile at her.

"You did not," Loni attempted to return his grin, but she was so numb she didn't know if it worked.

"He didn't. I did," She heard her dad's voice next and turned her head to find Luca and Kit on the other side of her bed. Lissa was sitting in a chair by the window and looked tired but gave Loni a smile and came to sit on the edge of her bed.

"That I believe," Loni said in a scratchy voice.

"Here, honey," Kit used the remote to raise the head part of the bed slightly. Then held up a glass of water for her. "Sip this slow. You've been out for a while."

"Thanks," Loni took a few sips. Her throat felt so numb she spilled a lot down her chin. Then she realized Manny was seeing this, and her eyes widened with horror.

"I look horrible, I'm sure," she muttered.

"That's not even possible," Manny said as he squeezed her hand.

"How do you feel, Loni?" Lissa asked.

"Numb and groggy mostly. Did the surgery go okay?"

"Yes," Luca said, but his voice sounded slightly off. She looked at him with questioning eyes, but he only offered her a small smile back. "We'll talk more about all that tomorrow, pumpkin."

"Your dad's right; it's late," Kit agreed.

"Why am I so tired? I just woke up," Loni whined.

"Right? Lazy kid. You act like your chest was cut open or something," Luca said dryly, earning a short giggle from Loni.

"Thanks dad for letting Manny come," she said and Luca reached over to squeeze her arm.

"I wish I could've brought my guitar. Tomorrow during the day, maybe," Manny offered. "I'm working on a little something."

"You got your guitar back?"

"Actually, your dad did," Manny smiled at her and then looked at Luca. "Thanks, Luca. I don't know how I can ever repay you, though..."

"You'll pay me back when you're a famous musician," Luca said.

"I don't know about that." Manny chuckled. "But it's nice to lose myself in my music again."

"I miss drawing so much," Loni mused. "I could try drawing from the bed, maybe? Could someone bring my stuff here?"

"Sure, I'll have Carly bring it over tomorrow," Kit agreed.

"How is Lucky doing? I miss him so much."

"He had a rough night, but when I left, he was happy playing with Stone," Manny said.

"He's at Grandpa's house with you guys?"

"It was my idea," Lissa came closer with her phone. Kit scooted over so she could sit closer and show Loni the photos Ruthie had sent her of Lucky. "He was looking for you and upset in the house. Grandpa and Manny promised to take good care of him."

"I'll make sure he's happy," Manny agreed. "He's a great dog."

"Thank you. He really is. He's probably so upset without me," Loni sniffled.

"None of that now," Luca cut in. "Lucky will be fine, but I'll try and talk your doctors into letting Manny bring him some afternoon."

"Luca," Kit said urgently, "they'll never allow that. Don't get her hopes up."

"He's an old dog and well-behaved." Her dad had that determined voice; he'd do whatever it took. "I'll make it happen."

She couldn't wait; she missed Lucky so much, and it hurt to be away from him. He was as much her best friend as Andrea was, maybe even more so.

Loni leaned back against her pillow and yawned.

"It's okay, Loni; if you're tired, go ahead and sleep," Manny offered. "I'll be back right away in the morning."

"Manny, you don't have to spend your whole summer at the hospital," Loni protested. "I'm sure you have other things to do."

"Since Leo's is closed right now, I don't," Manny countered.

"Sorry about that, kid," Luca offered. "Stone may need some help at the Grill, though."

"Yeah, he mentioned that, and I might help some at night. I want to be here during the day." Manny glanced at Loni. "Until you kick me out anyway."

"Never gonna happen," Loni squeezed his hand again. "Can you.. can we pretend we're somewhere else?"

"Of course," he spoke quietly. "Where should we go?"

"Camping," Loni closed her eyes and smiled softly. "We go to the lake every year in our camper. But I always wanted to try roughing it in a tent."

"Ewe, why bugs and the ground," Lissa commented, "yuck."

"Well, you aren't coming, so oh well."

"I am too! Mom!"

Kit laughed out loud. "Lissa, you don't need to go with her on her imaginary camping trip."

"I'd like her there. Keep them at least a foot apart," Luca piped in.

"Luca, it's--" Kit just laughed instead of finishing her statement.

"Ha! So I'm going," Lissa declared.

"Ugh, fine," Loni whined, but she couldn't help but he was amused at her little sister's persistence.

"Okay," Manny agreed. "So we're at a clearing in the woods. Lissa, can you look for sticks for a fire? Dry ones."

"On it!" Lissa cheered.

"She runs off to look while I take the tent out of the bag."

"Tents," Luca corrected him. "One for you and one for the girls."

"Dad," Loni whined, "you're ruining it!"

"Two tents," Manny said as his cheeks flushed. "I get them out and start setting up. But realize I have no idea what I'm doing."

Loni laughed. "Hold on! I'll help."

"Do you know how to do this?" Manny asked her.

"I know you to find out!" Loni said, "I pull up my phone and google how to set up a tent. Once I find the video, we watch it."

"That's cheating," Luca commented.

"Is not!" Lissa defended.

"It's not roughing it if you bring technology."

"Just cause they didn't have phones when you were a kid," Lissa said haughtily.

"You missed out, life was good when we used our imaginations instead of staring at screens all day."

"No one wants to hear about the dark ages right now," Lissa whined.

Kit cracked up laughing and Loni found herself softly laughing too.

"How old do you think I am!?"

"Like a hundred," Lissa giggled, and he pulled a face at her. "At least."

"Watch it, Shorty," Luca mock scolded her.

"While they argued over phones, Loni and I got both tents set up," Manny offered as he grinned at Loni.

"They look perfect," Loni closed her eyes for a moment. She could envision the clearing and the tents even feel the crunchy leaves under her feet.

"Ours is pink," Lissa offered.

"Of course it is." Loni smiled.

"I came back with like a thousand sticks for a fire!" Lissa added.

"That'll keep us warm all night," Manny enthused.

"Now, let's see if you can make a fire without your phones," Luca said.

"Easy! I know how to do this," Manny said. "I put the bigger sticks in the middle with some dry bark. Then I make a tent shape around the bigger sticks with small dry ones. Fill in the gaps with bark and then light a piece of paper to get it going. ...And whoosh! It all lights up at first but settles into a nice fire."

"Good job," Kit offered, and Loni opened her eyes to see her mom smiling softly.

Loni could almost see and smell it. "I plop on a log beside the fire, and Lucky sits by me."

"Marshmallow time!" Lissa declared. "I sit on the ground by the fire and set up my sixer."

"Your what?" Manny asked.

"Lissa always liked to roast six at once, so she'd look for the longest but skinniest stick she could find. Called it a sixer," Loni explained and Manny chuckled.

"Alright, let's all set up our sixers then!" Manny chirped.

"I'll find three!" Lissa cheered, Loni was finding her enthusiasm contagious and glad she 'came along' now.

"So you're eating marshmallows for dinner?" Kit asked, and this time Luca laughed.

"You're scolding them on what they're eating while pretend camping?" Luca questioned.

"I can't help it," Kit laughed softly. "Always mothering."

"I found a pot roast my mom snuck in my bag and set it on the fire," Loni said to appease Kit.

"An entire pot roast?" Luca laughed again. "In your bag?"

"Quiet, daddio!" Lissa scolded him. "While that's heating up, tell us a scary story, Manny."

"Uh I don't think I should get Loni spooked."

Kit and Luca both chuckled as Loni smirked lightly.

"Ghost stories never scare me, I can always guess them."

"Alright then," Manny shrugged and then leaned in. "They say this very campsite is haunted. Anyone that's ever camped here has run off in a hurry, getting spooked by things."

"Like what?" Loni asked as she stifled another yawn.

"Strange noises and voices, but no one there to make them," Manny said quietly.

"It is haunted," Lissa whispered as she huddled closer to Loni.

"Or someone left their phone on," Luca cut in.

"Luca," Kit scolded him.

"There's a twist though," Loni guessed. "It's not going to be haunted."

"Loni stop guessing during the story," Kit scolded her this time. "Go on, Manny."

"Then the kids went missing," Manny said in a deeper voice. "One moment they were there and then gone, just like that, no trace. After that no one would stay there anymore, until one day, a kid was on a walk and stumbled upon the site. One moment he was alone, and then suddenly, someone was there.."

"Who!?" Lissa asked.

"Another kid, but his clothes were old fashioned, and he spoke strangely."

"A ghost," Lissa guessed.

"Too obvious," Loni mumbled.

Manny just shrugged. "So, the kid asks the strange kid who he is and where he came from. He starts talking about his house and how it was right there and he keeps asking where's my house?"

"Like he thinks his house was just there?" Loni asked.

"Right." Manny nodded. "He said he was heading home and his house is gone."

"He introduces himself as Timmy and the other kid in the story is unnamed but we'll call him Dan," Manny continued. "Dan doesn't feel any bad intentions from Timmy so he suggests maybe he found the wrong spot, and they walk around trying to find the house."

"But Timmy is a ghost!" Lissa exclaimed.

"He's a friendly ghost," Kit offered.

"Not a ghost," Loni added as she yawned again.

"The boys sought out to look for Timmy's house and as they walked on they felt like they were walking in circles. They kept returning to the same campsite that Timmy insisted should be where his house is..."

As Manny continued to tell the story, exhaustion took its toll on Loni, his words didn't register anymore, just the soothing tone of his voice, and warm feel of her hand in his. As sleep took over, a soft smile graced her face.

Chapter 14

The next morning Loni woke to soft voices in her room.

"Why are you here so early? It's not even six," her mom was saying.

"Dr. Morgan is testing the twins this morning. Andre is bringing them to the cafeteria now to get a bite to eat first. Where's Luca?" Aunt Carly answered.

"He headed to our on-call room to shower," Kit explained. "We all slept in here again last night."

"I see that," Carly's heels clicked as she walked across the floor.

"Thanks for bringing her sketchbook," Kit said. "Any little things we can do to fill her days, make her smile..."

"Whatever I can do, I will," Carly said softly.

"Carly, you're shaking! Don't worry; the twins will be okay."

"What if they aren't, though? What if one of them has this thing?"

"Then you'll have caught it early," Kit said assuredly. "We could've done things for Loni if we knew sooner."

"Kit, I just can't imagine going through what you are!" Carly sobbed at the end, and her mom quickly hushed her.

"It's okay. It's going to be okay," Kit said in a low voice.

"You shouldn't be the one comforting me," Carly's voice was muffled. "Especially after last night."

Last night? Loni remained still, hoping she'd reveal more.

"Carly, you ready?" She heard Andre's voice and then a sniffling Carly sighed, "As ready as I will be."

"Come on, sweetheart. It'll be okay," Andre said as Loni heard Carly's heels clicking away.

"How's our favorite patient today?" Loni heard Dr. Morgan's voice next.

"Still sleeping," Kit said as Loni opened her eyes. "Or not, morning, honey."

"Morning," Loni said as she looked around. Lissa was passed out in the bed next to her, and the big chair in the room had a blanket draped over it.

Dr. Morgan came over to check her vitals. "How are you feeling this morning, Loni?"

"I'm not in any pain, kind of numb," Loni admitted.

"You're on a lot of pain medication right now," Dr. Morgan assured her. "It'll leave you feeling a little groggy and numb."

"I'm hungry," Loni said with a note of surprise. She hadn't been in so long!

"That's great news!"

"You're awake, morning, Pumpkin," Luca stepped in next; he was freshly showered but had huge bags under his eyes, so did her mom.

"What's great news?" Luca asked as he walked over to squeeze her hand.

"Loni said she's feeling hungry today," Kit explained.

"I dreamed about my mom's pot roast."

Luca and Kit both chuckled softly.

"Well, it won't be that, but I'll ask the cafeteria to prepare breakfast for you. I need to get next door for some testing. Dr. Blake Sr. will be here soon, though. Junior will be in this afternoon too. He's on for the night shift," Dr. Morgan explained. "I think we can all sit down and talk at that time."

Loni looked up curiously, she knew things were bad. One part of her wanted them to rip the Band-Aid off and just tell her. The other part of her wasn't ready to hear it. At least she had some time to prepare for what she assumed was the worst.

"That sounds good," Luca said carefully as he sat down. Lissa woke up at that moment with a loud annoyed groan.

"What time is it?" She huffed as she sat up and stretched

"Time for you three to go home and get some rest," Dr. Morgan said with a slight grin.

"We'll head over to the on-call room for a nap soon," Kir offered.

"Nope. I'm kicking you three out and don't want you back here until at least noon today. You all look like zombies."

"But—" Luca protested.

"I've been lenient," she reminded him. "But I told you, you need to take care of yourselves too. Loni is fine here. Dr. Blake will be here soon. Go. Now."

"We can't just leave-" Kit argued this time.

"Mom, Dad, please go home and take a nap. I'm fine, I swear," Loni begged.

"But Pumpkin-"

"Dad, go! And check on Lucky, too, please."

"Speaking of that—" Luca looked at Dr. Morgan. "A visit from her dog would make her day..."

"You'll have to talk Dr. Gupta into that," Dr. Morgan grinned. "Now come on, let's go. I've made your brother and sister-in-law wait long enough."

Later that morning, Loni felt fairly good. She'd eaten breakfast and had been able to keep it down. The pain medicine was keeping her pain at bay, and the nurses said she looked to be healing well from the surgery.

"Hi, Loni." The tall doctor she vaguely recalled from last night had entered her room.

"Morning, Dr. Blake Sr, right?" Loni questioned.

"You can just call me John. It's easier," he said as he came over to take her vitals. "Or Gus's dad."

She giggled at that, "Gus looks a lot like you."

"Yeah, we always had a tight bond." John smiled.

"Is it weird for you that he's my mom's brother?" Loni asked.

"It was...unexpected. I'll say that much."

"Did you know my mom was out there?"

"Not until later down the road, it was at a time that Stacey and I were having other issues. We separated and then divorced, and I'm ashamed to admit I never pushed her to reconnect with your mom."

"You don't have to be ashamed of that."

"I am, though. I just wanted to move on from the marriage and for things to be amicable, but that wasn't fair to my kids. They deserved to know they had an older sister out there."

"Kids more than Gus?" Loni questioned

Loni was so excited about the idea of having more family around. Maybe they could even go with on the family's summer trip to the lake. Hopefully she got to go on the trip this year.

"Enough about all that for now. I heard you tried some breakfast this morning?"

"Oatmeal and an apple," Loni said with a smile. "It's been an hour, and still down."

"That's great news. The ventricle repair I did should make you feel quite a bit better over the next coming days," John told her. "However, with your heart beating at it's full capacity again, we must be extra weary of your heart condition. If your heart starts beating too fast at any time, you hit that alarm immediately, got it?"

"Got it," Loni agreed.

"Knock, knock," Her grandpa said as he walked in and Loni smiled wide to see Manny was behind him.

"Come on in," Loni said as they stepped further into the room.

"We're all done for now. If you get tired, kick these guys out and get some rest, okay?"

"Okay, John, thanks," Loni smiled.

John looked curiously at Stone briefly, then the two men nodded at each other, and then John left.

"So, how ya feeling today?" Stone asked as he came over and squeezed her shoulder.

"Better than I have since I got here," Loni said. "I even ate breakfast."

"That's great, Loni," Manny said as he came to sit on her other side. She noticed he had his guitar, and her grin widened. Was he going to play it for her?

"How is Lucky doing?"

"Better," Stone said. "Smart of Lissa to suggest the change of house. They came by to see him today, and he was so excited. He nearly licked your dad's face off."

Loni giggled at the image, she was Lucky's favorite person for sure, but her dad was a close second.

"It's funny, I begged my mom my whole life for a dog, and she always said no. Said, Manny, they're too much work and their dirty, and they drool.." his voice became higher pitched as he mocked his mom. "But you should see her now! She can't get enough of Lucky."

Stone laughed heartily in agreement. "Those two sure have bonded. Seeing your mom smile after she didn't get that job is nice."

"Yeah, she was really hoping for that," Manny sighed. "I'm glad you have work for her at the Grill, though."

"Maybe she could also come work for Leo's once it's open again?" Loni suggested, and Manny winced.

"I love my mom but don't want to work with her."

Stone laughed out loud, "Understandable. She can be a bit bossy, huh?"

Manny chuckled, "I'd say! She had your grandpa eating quinoa last night."

"No way!" Loni said as Stone shushed Manny.

"Good thing my daughter didn't hear that she'll join in and make it worse," Stone scolded.

"I won't tell," Loni promised and he ruffled her hair.

"I'll leave you two kids to visit. Holler if you need me!"

"Okay, Grandpa!" Loni called after him.

"I'm so glad you're feeling a little better," Manny said. "You sound more like your cheerful self."

"John, the doctor that did my surgery, said I should feel a little better over the next few days," Loni said. "I know there's more to the story than that, though. Neither of my parents looked like they slept at all. Plus, Dr. Morgan said something about a meeting this afternoon."

"Just keep positive," Manny suggested. "You feel good right now; enjoy that."

"You're so right," she agreed.

"Hey, Loni!" Andrea walked in holding up a card; she brought it over to sit at her end table. "Hey, Manny."

"How are you feeling today?" Andrea asked.

"Good, actually, I won't barf on you this time," Loni said with a short laugh. "Come sit down."

"I can't stay today," Andrea said regretfully. "A bunch of us are going to the beach. It's supposed to hit eighty today. Can you believe it?"

"No, it's always the same temperature here," Loni joked.

"Right.. uh, well, everyone signed that for you," Andrea offered.

"Thanks, that was sweet," Loni said.

"Sure! Even Garret signed it. He's going to be at the beach today. Can you believe it? He's a junior! Kelly thinks he likes me."

"Oh wow," Loni bit back an urge to tell Andrea to be careful. Garret had a major reputation.

"Right? Well, I better go, but I'll stop in later this week again, okay?"

"Sure. Have fun," Loni said as Andrea smiled and hurried out.

"That was so rude!" Manny looked at the doorway with an irritated look in his eyes.

"What?"

"If she wasn't going to visit you, why come at all? To brag about a beach day?"

"I don't think she meant to do that," Loni excused.

"Maybe not, but still," he muttered as he picked up her card. "Everyone signed it, but no one can come to see you?"

"They've always been more Andrea's friends than mine," Loni explained. "I kind of feel like we're fading apart."

"I'm sorry," Manny said softly. "I had that happen with a good friend once. He fell in with a really bad crowd; they were drinking a lot, doing drugs, and getting into trouble. I promised my mom I'd never do stuff like that. So I had to distance myself."

"That must've been hard," Loni took his hand, and he squeezed it gently.

"It was," Manny agreed. "But I'm glad I did it; if I fell in with them, who knows where I'd be right now."

"Well, I'm glad you're right here with me," Loni said as a slight blush touched her cheeks.

"So am I," Manny said, returning her grin.

"Are you sure, though? It's summer. You're supposed to have fun like Andrea and her friends."

"I am having fun," Manny said, and Loni gave him a look at that.

"Well, the waiting room sucks," he confessed with a laugh. "But when I'm in here with you, I'm having fun."

"I'm not going to believe imaginary dates and pretend camping trips are better than the real thing, Manny."

"Loni, with you they are," he squeezed her hand and softly ran his thumb over the front. "I'd rather go on a thousand imaginary dates with you than a real one with anyone else."

She felt her belly explode with little butterflies. "Really? That's so sweet. I—thank you."

"No need to thank me, it's just the truth."

"Even if Lissa tags along on some of our imaginary dates?"

"Even if." Manny chuckled. "At least she got spooked by my scary story."

"Oh, I need to hear the rest of that! I fell asleep."

"Next time we go fake camping." He let go of her hand, and she missed the warmth immediately, but she no longer minded when she saw him picking up his guitar.

"You're going to play for me?"

"Just the melody I've been working on. I'm not ready to share the words yet." He blushed a little, and she was instantly curious.

He strummed a few times to get the tune he liked and then started playing a catchy melody. She watched his face as he played. A slight smile lifted his lips, and his green eyes looked dreamy.

"That was amazing," she breathed out when he finished, and he beamed proudly.

"Yeah, you think so?"

"I do," she agreed. "But I really want to hear the words you wrote."

"It's just a start and cheesy and embarrassing," he said sheepishly.

"You have been seeing me every day at my absolute worst. You have no reason to be embarrassed about anything."

"This, I do," he laughed nervously. "I'm not joking. It's so cheesy."

"Manny, please?" She looked at him with the pout that always worked on her dad, assuming he'd laugh at her. Instead, his gaze softened, and he sighed.

"Okay, I'll sing it to you, but you can't laugh, okay?"

"I'd never," she promised him.

He took a nervous breath and started playing again. She found her gaze transfixed on his face, but he avoided her eye contact.

Finally, he started singing.

"Life's been rough for a while.""Stuck in the dark all the time.""Never thought I'd find a place that could be mine." "Cue the girl with the pretty eyes." "She could light up the darkest night." "There's the girl with the warmest smile.""It's aimed at me, and now my world's alive."

Loni was transfixed as he sang, her eyes teary and a soft smile on her lips.

"That's all I got right now," he said sheepishly as he stopped playing. "It's okay to laugh. I know I said not to, but—"

"That was beautiful, Manny," she breathed out.

"You really liked it?"

"I loved it."

More then loved it. If she weren't stuck in this bed, she'd be dancing all over the hospital right now!

"Yeah?" He set his guitar down and scooted closer to her bedside. "It's true, you know. Every part of it."

He paused for a moment, a hand coming to rest gently against her cheek.

"Life's been rough since my mom lost her job. After we left our last town, I said I wasn't even going to bother trying to make friends. Then I saw you, and you smiled at me, and it was like nothing I ever felt. You made me feel so warm and welcome."

"You should've always felt welcome anywhere." She frowned.

"I never felt that way. I never felt like I belonged anywhere until now."

"Well, you do belong here. Don't ever forget it," she said.

"You're the sweetest girl I've ever known," he said as he softly trailed his fingertips over her cheek. "The day we met, Leo's was full of kids. Tons of guys our age. I don't know how or why I got so lucky that you smiled at me, but I'll never get tired of seeing it."

"Stop! You're making me blush so much," she giggled.

"You're pretty when you blush," he whispered.

"Now you're making my heart race and it's not supposed to."

"Are you okay?" his face became alarmed.

"Fine," she assured him fast. "Just a little heart patient humor. It's not anything bad just a fluttery feeling."

"I get that every time I see you," he confessed.

Crap, he could maybe make her swoon and joking aside probably shouldn't...

"You know, that was my first day helping my dad," Loni said. "I came out to get a soda and saw the cutest guy I'd ever seen. I noticed Kelly eyeing you and figured you'd look over there soon. But you didn't; you looked around, all nervous. I didn't think a good-looking guy like you would have anything to be nervous about. So I smiled at you to let you know not to be."

"Well, it worked," he said. "Sort of; in some ways, I was more nervous. Just cause I liked you so much."

"I think I'm the lucky one because Kelly is a bombshell, but you saw me first-"

"Kelly doesn't even come close," he insisted, "Loni, you're beautiful, and not just on the outside. You're a beautiful person. I am so lucky I know you."

Her eyes were welled with tears. "Manny... thank you."

"I'm pretty crazy about you, in case that wasn't obvious."

"I'm pretty crazy about you too," she said softly.

"Can I.." his hand slipped down her cheek to softly graze her neck.

"Can you what?" She whispered.

"I wish I could kiss you, but I figure with your oxygen I probably can't, but could I kiss your cheek?" He looked as nervous as he did when he played her the song earlier.

"Yes," she said in a squeakier voice than she meant.

He leaned over and slowly but softly pressed his lips against her cheek. She closed her eyes and relished the warm and tingly feeling of his lips on her skin. He allowed his lips to linger there for a long moment. Then slowly pulled away, and their eyes locked.

"I can't wait to take you on a real date and give you a real kiss goodnight."

"I can't wait either." Her cheek tingled from where he'd kissed her.

"Whoa, lady, where you going? You can't go in there!" She heard her grandpa's voice and saw a white-haired woman entering her room. Her grandpa ran up behind her, and she whirled around to face him.

"Holy -" Stone's eyes widened in shock. "Stacey? The hell happened to you?"

Stacey!? As in, her mom's mother?

"Not now, Stone," she spoke in a low and quiet voice. "Please give me a moment with...our granddaughter, okay?"

Stone looked hesitant to leave.

"I'll only be a moment," Stacey said.

"It's okay, Grandpa," Loni assured him, then glanced at Manny. "Can you give us a second?"

"Yeah, of course. If you need me, just yell out, okay?" He said as he stood, and she nodded.

The woman, Stacey, was looking in wonder at the walls. "This purple flower... you dreamed of it?"

"Yeah.. a whole field of them, why? How did you know that?"

She walked over and sat where Manny has just been sitting. Loni noticed she had a sketchbook, and she opened it.

"My daughter, London, liked to draw too," she said as Loni looked at the pages of purple flowers. "There was this field of flowers we used to go to on her birthday. Eventually, the purple ones took over."

"Aster Celeste's do that; some consider them a weed," Loni watched as she flipped the pages and took in all the drawings of flowers. "I think they're too pretty to be called that."

"You know your stuff," Stacey chuckled softly. "I never even knew what they were called. So they call you Loni, short for Leondra?"

"Yes, I'm named after my grandpa Leo."

"It's beautiful, Leondra. I don't like using short names, so I hope you don't mind if I call you that."

"I don't mind at all," Loni said. "So London likes to draw flowers too?"

"Loved it," Stacey said, "you two had that in common."

"I guess so," Loni wondered where London was; would she come to see her too?

"This was her favorite." Stacey flipped to the second to last page. It was full of colors and flowers, all bending into one abstract design.

"It's beautiful!" Loni breathed out as she gazed at it.

Stacey stunned her by carefully removing the page and handing it to Loni. "I think she'd like you to have this one."

"Me? I couldn't take this! It's beautiful; this could win an award or—"

"Or inspire you. Keep it, please."

"Where is she? I'd like to ask her to be certain."

"Trust me on this, I know she'd," Stacey stopped when footsteps interrupted them.

"Loni," Kit gasped as she and Luca walked in. They both stopped short when they saw Stacey at her bedside.

"I was just leaving, Cricket. I'm sorry I intruded, but I wanted to see her." Stacey sighed softly as she gazed at Loni's face, and then she stood.

"Don't ever give up on your dreams, Leondra. Not ever, and don't let anyone get in your way. I shouldn't have gotten in her way. But maybe—" She took a breath and continued. "Maybe now you can live out those dreams for you and her."

"What do you mean?"

A tear slid down Stacey's cheek, and she quickly patted Loni's shoulder and stood.

She then walked up to her stunned parents and said, "I know what London would want, and this is it. Tell Johnathan I've agreed."

Kit let out a sob, and Luca breathed out, "Thank you."

She then hurried out of the room.

"What did she mean?" Loni looked at her parents with confusion in her eyes.

"We have a lot to talk about, honey," Kit said with teary eyes.

Chapter 15

Gus was hustling into the hospital when a voice stopped him. He turned to find Jenny walking quickly toward him, her jet-black hair whipping in the wind. He'd got in late the night before, and the toll everything weighed heavy, causing him to sleep in. In the past, he'd have unloaded his burdens on her. However, lately, they'd been at such a crossroads it was easier to avoid her.

"I can't right now. I don't have time," Gus stammered as she grew closer.

"You've been avoiding me," she accused. "Ignoring my calls. What am I supposed to do, Gus? I can't sit in limbo."

"I know, I get it. You just don't understand. A lot is going on right now."

"There is always going to be a lot going on; that's not the problem here."

"Of course it is. You hate that I'm busy. You hate my career—"

"No, that's not what I hate."

"Yes, it is it, Jenny."

"No, I hate that you won't find time for us within your busy career. Not, can't, Gus, won't. Because if you tried hard enough, you could."

"Jenny—"

"No. Let me finish for once; let me have one second of your precious time to set myself free."

"What?"

"It's over, Gus. You don't have to worry about avoiding me anymore. You can have the apartment. My sister offered me a room at her house for now."

"Jenny, don't..."

"I can't sit around waiting for you to decide to be a decent boyfriend or break up with me. It's not fair to me."

"I'm sorry. I am. I- let's not do it like this," he pleaded. "Let's sit down and talk; let's—"

"Talk about what? Why drag this out?"

"I.. damn it. I didn't want to break up in the hospital's parking lot!" He brushed his hair back with a frustrated sigh.

"It's fitting in a way. You don't even have time for the breakup." Her almond-shaped, piercing dark eyes, which always seemed to see right into his soul, were dimmed as if she'd shut herself off him. She looked at the hospital behind him with a wry smile. "This hospital is the one you were married to and always will be. I hope it's worth it in the end."

"I'm sorry."

"Said with no emotion," she sighed. "Did you ever love me?"

"Of course I did. I mean I do!" This was going horribly and he was feeling crummier by the moment.

"You said it right the first time. At least you did at one point." She sounded so defeated and yet he couldn't deny it. When did he fall out of love with her? He was unsure where they stood and if they could continue on, but he thought he still loved her, he thought that's why he was holding on but as he stood there he realized it had faded. He forgot that relationships are a living breathing thing, if neglected for too long they die.

"Goodbye. Gus," she said as she turned to leave. He simply watched her walk away. He didn't chase after her; he didn't see the point. His heart felt heavy and his stomach was balled up in knot knowing it was all his fault. Jenny was acting strong but he knew her. She'd go home and cry and it'd be all his fault, he felt like such a tool.

"You've turned into your father."

"Excuse me?" He turned around to find his mom walking towards him. London's old sketchbook gripped firmly in her hands. "How long were you out here listening?"

"Long enough."

"You shouldn't have been."

"On the contrary I wish I'd been more involved in your life sooner. You just let a fantastic woman walk away."

"This was a long time coming, mom," Gus said, "and like I said, none of your business."

"Career isn't everything, Gus," Stacey replied curtly. "Learn from this mistake so you don't end up alone."

"You think keeping myself at arm's length is something I learned from Dad?" Gus shot back.

She flinched from his harsh words. It was too late, though, he'd opened the gate, and before he knew it, all those pent-up words came barreling out at her.

"You'd never told him anything. You always held back from him, me, hell even London at times. You'd get sad, withdraw for days, and refuse to tell us why. How was he supposed to stay with a woman who only gave him half of herself? How was I supposed to learn to open up when you never did?"

"I tried, I did, but I couldn't — I couldn't talk about her." Stacey's voice was full of all the emotion she never showed Gus, which stunned him. He went silent as he listened. "I knew he'd hate me. I knew you'd all would. I couldn't lose you and your sister's respect and love. I didn't want you to hate me like Cricket did- or does."

"She doesn't hate you," Gus said, his voice slightly softer. "I don't know my sister that well yet, but she's not hateful."

"How could she not? I abandoned her."

"Why?" Gus had to ask; he had to know. "Why did you leave her?"

"I was so young. My parents were so angry I was pregnant, to begin with. I told Stone to take us away, far, far away. I said we'd start over and be a little family... but-"

"But what?"

"It was all wrong, from the very start. I never got that magical connection with her they'd talk about. She'd never stop fussing or crying for me. But when Stone would pick her up, she was the happiest baby ever. I felt so worthless with her, sometimes I honestly felt like she hated me. Over time, I felt so suffocated at home. I started to drink, but I hid it from Stone. I'd throw away the bottles in the neighbor's garbage. I knew I shouldn't have been drinking; even Stone had cut back on weed and beer with a baby in the house. I couldn't, though; it was the only way I could cope."

"Mom," Gus's voice broke as a tear slid down his cheek. "That sounds like postpartum depression. No wonder you used alcohol to cope. You needed help."

"Maybe it was, but all I knew then was that I had a baby that hated me and a boyfriend who was always working at the bar. Then one day it wasn't even noon and I was wasted. I thought Cricket was upstairs napping. I went into the kitchen to refill my drink, and there she was on the floor with a butcher knife." She shuddered, and Gus could tell the memory was vivid for her. "I left that night."

"That must have been horrifying for you." Gus felt a new understanding wash over him. "Did you ever seek help?"

"No, Gus," she confessed tearfully. "I continued to drink myself numb until I got arrested one night."

"Arrested!?"

She nodded sadly, "My dad picked me up and took me straight to rehab. The only good thing that man ever did for me..."

She trailed off as her eyes filled with pain. She never spoke about her parents. Gus and London had never even met them. He didn't even know if they were still alive.

"Anyway, I met your dad not long after that, and it was a second chance for me at life. I jumped on it and tried to hide my shameful past."

"Did you ever tell Kit this?"

"Some of it. I don't know how much she believed me. Her argument is I never came back, and she's right; I didn't. I broke my little girl's heart and I'll never forgive myself. I have a hard time even looking at her. It fills me with regret and shame."

"And you told her on the call that you never wanted to know her or her to know us?"

"Only because I was afraid I'd lose you. I hate myself for that call. It was so brave for her to reach out, and I dismissed her."

"You wouldn't have lost me," Gus countered. "I was what, ten at that time? I might've been confused and angry initially, but I'd have understood eventually. London was so young she'd have just been happy to have a big sister."

"You'd have never seen me the same. When your dad found out, he looked at me with absolute disgust, and you always reacted so similarly to him. You were always looking for a reason to pick him over me."

"Because you always picked her. I was second in your eyes; we all were. London was everything to you. I accepted it, Mom. I didn't get it, but I accepted it. It was easier to live with Dad and focus on my future than live with you and feel like second best all the time."

"You were never second best," she gasped in horror. "I just- she- she was my best friend. She was my second chance. She - my baby girl. And —"

She started to break into sobs, and Gus took a step closer. "Mom, it's okay; I'm sorry."

"...And now she's going to be gone forever. I told them I'd do it. I told Cricket and her husband they could have her heart. I will lose her... just like I always knew I would."

"You did!? You- really?" He stopped talking and pulled his frail mom into his arms. "This is the right thing, Mom. You're doing the right thing. You'll be okay, we'll all be okay."

She sobbed softly as he comforted her, his earlier anger all but forgotten.

Loni was trying hard to comprehend what her mom and dad had told her, and she couldn't wrap her head around it. Dr. Morgan and John had come while Kit and Luca explained everything, to Loni. They chimed in from time to time, to clarify certain things.

They wanted to remove her heart and replace it with her aunt's heart.

How? How could she ever do that? It meant that London would die. John tearfully explained she'd already passed, but Loni had difficulty understanding that.

She felt tears stream down her face, and Kit and Luca rushed to her bed. Her dad pulled her into his arms and held her as her mom rubbed her back.

"Shh, I know, honey. I know how scary this all this," Kit soothed her.

"How can she be dead if she's alive to give me her heart?" Loni pulled herself away from Luca and addressed her question to the doctors. "What if she could wake up?"

"She has been on life support for six years, " John said slowly. "There is no way for her brain to recover from the damage it took. We should have let her off life support years ago, but. Well, that doesn't matter; what does matter is now it doesn't have to be for nothing. London can continue, in a way, through you."

"But.."

"You'll get the best part of her." Gus had stepped inside the room now, and Loni looked up to see him. "She had the world's biggest and kindest heart. I'm so glad that part of her can live on."

"Really?" Loni sniffled back more tears. "But she's your sister and she'll be gone."

"She's been gone," Gus said as he walked over and sat on the edge of her bed. "And it's been hard, but now I have another sister and two nieces. That makes me so happy; you have no idea. I can't wait to get to know you all more, but I don't want all our time to be in hospitals, Loni. I want to see you thrive."

"We all do," Kit added as she squeezed her arm.

"If I don't do this, then what?" Loni asked. "Does that mean I'd die?"

"You will need a heart replacement sooner than later," John spoke up. "There is a temporary fix we can do to buy you time. But it isn't perfect and comes with it's own set of risks.

It could be years before another compatible donor would become available."

Meaning someone else would have to die; she shuddered at the thought.

"Meanwhile, London will have to come off life support soon," John continued. "Whether she gives you her heart or not. A person can't stay on it indefinitely."

"London's organs won't only save you," Dr. Morgan added. "She'll help a lot of other people."

Loni swallowed back a thick lump in her throat. "I guess I understand. I'm just very freaked out."

"We all are," Luca said as he squeezed her arm.

"Will this change .. what I feel? I won't have my own heart anymore?"

"No, Loni. I know I said you're getting the best part of her, and you are. But technically, your heart is not where all your memories, feelings, and personality are stored," Gus explained. "You will still be you."

Loni suddenly felt silly for asking that. Of course, it wouldn't change who she was. She didn't know why she thought that. Yet Gus was so calm and kind about it, she really appreciated that.

"But people have talked about feeling a connection to their donor after," Dr Morgan offered. "Some even become friendly with the donor's family."

"Really?" Loni perked up some at that.

"I think that, in some ways, you're already connected," Kit said as she ran a hand softly through Loni's hair. "You had the dream of the flower field she used to go to. I think her spirit has been watching out for you, waiting until it was time to help you."

Kit looked at the doctors and wiped a few tears from her cheeks. "I know that's not possible, but I feel it."

"I believe you; not everything can be defined with science," John agreed.

"I do, too," Gus said, offering Kit a soft smile. "The art and flowers, they have so much in common."

Loni felt a deep sadness overcome her. "It would have been so amazing to have had an aunt that loved drawing too. We could've sat side by side in the field of flowers and painted them together."

"Maybe, you can go there after, and see it for yourself," Gus said softly. "I go there sometimes. I can show you where it is."

"I'd like that," Loni whispered.

"Well then we need to get you fixed up so you can go," John said his voice a bit rough.

"What happens next?" Loni asked as she took a brave but shaky breath.

"You'll need some time to recover from your current surgery," John explained. "London will be transferred here. Once you're able to handle the surgery, her surgery and yours will happen at the same time. This is so her heart can be transferred to you as soon as we possibly can."

"Can you do this surgery? Isn't it like a conflict of interest or whatever?" Luca asked John.

"Loni isn't blood-related to me, I can because of that clause. Technically I should opt-out. Touching my own daughter's heart is a major grey area. But, I don't want anyone else operating on Loni. This is too crucial. It all has to be done right."

"What about you, Dr. Morgan?" Loni asked. "You won't do the surgery?"

"I'm the head of the cardiology department; my role is to develop a plan for the patient. Be it drugs or surgery. While I have performed many heart surgeries, my expertise isn't focused on that. Whereas Dr. Blake, on the other hand, is the top heart surgeon in the country. He's performed countless heart surgeries, including transplants. I will be right there to assist him the entire time. We will call in another team to do London's surgery as we will have them harvest her other organs as well."

"Okay, " Loni nodded, it all made sense, yet it was still so scary and sad. The word harvest felt so awful.

"Can I see her before this all happen?" Loni asked. "London, I mean."

"Of course," John said. "She'll be moved here soon, and we'll bring you in to see her."

"You okay, Pumpkin?" Luca asked as he studied her carefully.

"Not really," Loni admitted.

"It's okay, honey," Kit said, "it's a lot to take in. Your dad and I aren't so okay either. But we'll get through this."

"We do have a little something that might help cheer you up some." Dr. Morgan waved at someone through the door as she spoke.

Loni's eyebrows raised as a wheelchair was brought into her room. "What's that for?"

"You're getting a little trip outside," Luca said with a slight smile on his otherwise tired face. "Ready to see the sun again?"

"Really? I get to go outside!" Loni did perk up at that as the doctors wheeled the chair over.

"For a little bit," John said. "We think a little fresh air will do you some good. We'll keep you on your oxygen but get you unhooked from the other machines. An hour a day will be fine for you to do this."

"Thank you so much! I can't wait, even the lobby will be great at this point," Loni said.

"It's your lucky day you get the lobby and the parking lot," Luca joked.

As Kit wheeled Loni to the elevator, her dad was texting someone. She felt there was more to this than just going outside, but she didn't want to set her hopes up.

When they got down to the main corridor, Loni was stunned at how busy it was. The waiting room was full of people, and many doctors hurriedly walked around. The upstairs wing she was in was always so quiet, what a difference.

Kit pushed her along to the big main doors, and Dr. Gupta was standing there. He offered them a big smile and a wink at Loni as they passed through.

Loni knew something was up then, but she took a moment to close her eyes and enjoy the sun on her face.

"Where are they?" Kit whispered to Luca.

"Coming now."

"What's going on?" Loni asked just as her grandpa's truck pulled up upfront.

Her eyes filled with happy tears at who was in the passenger seat.

"Lucky!"

Chapter 16

"Lucky!" Loni cheered again just as the dog saw her and started trying to jump out the slightly open window. "Oh my gosh! Oh, I'm so happy to see you too, my boy!"

"Stay calm!" Luca was rushing up to the truck.

"You talking to Loni or the dog?" Kit teased.

"Both." Luca tossed Loni a smile and then carefully opened the door, grabbing Lucky's leash to prevent him from jumping at her.

He jerked and whined, wanting at her, but Luca held tight until he calmed enough and then walked him over to a very anxious Loni.

"Oh, Lucky, my sweet old boy! I missed you so much!" She leaned down to pet him and tug his ears as he likes, and he grunted with happiness at her affections. "Did you miss me too?"

"Sure seems like he did!" Stone said as he got out of the truck to join them.

"Of course he did; you're his favorite person." Luca was smiling softly.

"And Lucky is my favorite thing ever." She spoke directly to Lucky as she began to scratch under his chin. "I'm going to be better soon, good boy, okay? I know you miss sleeping with me. I miss you too! My little feet warmer, you."

She felt happier than she had in days as she cooed at him and pet him. She still felt so awful about what they had to do to fix her heart, but the thought of spending time with Lucky again was helping her feel better about it.

She could even envision Lucky running through that flower field with her.

"Manny's been taking really good care of him," Stone knelt to give Lucky a pat on the head.

"Where is Manny?" Loni asked curiously.

"He and his mom are at the church. Your dad didn't want the food in the walk-in at Leo's to go to waste. What we couldn't freeze, we're donating," Stone explained.

"Oh, that's great, Dad! What a good idea!" Kit, enthused, she's knelt and started petting Lucky along with Loni. He loved the attention, and his tongue was flopping around happily.

"It was Manny's idea."

"He is a a good kid," Luca murmured.

"Isn't he?" Kit agreed.

"You lucked out. Could've been stuck with a Kyle," Stone told Luca.

"I did luck out. I deserved to get stuck with a Kyle," Luca chuckled.

"Oh, there's still Lissa, don't worry, I'm sure she'll bring home some real fun ones for ya," Stone offered, and her mom snorted back laughter.

"Can't wait," Luca said dryly.

Loni couldn't stop grinning. Her dad really liked Manny; and it felt so good to know that. It warmed her heart to picture them being close someday, just like her dad and grandpa.

She felt like her smile would burst off her face at that point.

Lissa had spent most of the day in the on-call room. Her mom and dad planned to talk to Loni about the heart transplant today. She knew it would be a hard conversation for everyone and thought it best to stay out of the way.

She hopped off the top bunk bed, landing softly on her feet. Grabbing a few bills from her dad's wallet, she left the room to head to the vending machines.

As she stepped into the corridor, she noticed the door to the old lab that Gus told her should hide in was slightly ajar. Curiosity got the better of her, and she quietly stepped into the room. She saw Gus in the corner with his head down.

"Uncle Gus? You okay?"

He jumped slightly as he turned towards her; she saw right away that his eyes were puffy and his cheeks were stained from recent tears. "I uh, sorry - should've shut the door. I didn't mean for anyone to find me in here."

"You don't have to be sorry for crying." She said as she walked towards him. "Everyone cries. Even my dad."

He blew his nose and let out a long sigh. "Doctors aren't supposed to. We're supposed to stay professional, respectful and kind but detached."

"Kind of impossible when it's family," Lissa commented.

"Kind of impossible always," he confessed. "I always get attached to my patients."

"I would too, I think," she said thoughtfully. "But if I was a patient. I would want the doctors to care about me. More reason to want to fix me."

Gus let out a small laugh, "we always care."

"You know what I meant!" Lissa gave him a look. "Want to talk about it?"

"Not really," he said with a wry smile. "But, I don't think you're going away, are you, little Ninja Girl?

"Nope," she chirped as she flopped down in a chair beside him. She found herself smiling at the pet name. "Ninja Girl is here to listen, like it or not."

"I suppose I should distract you, and keep the vending machines safe."

She rolled her eyes at that. "Is it London and what's going to happen to her that's got you upset?"

"A little, I don't go see her much anymore, but I'm sad I won't be able to soon," he admitted. "But more so, I'm relieved for her. She can finally find peace this way. Loni can have a chance at a long life. It's the best thing that could've happened. For everyone, but, my mom."

"You're worried about her?"

"Very," Gus confirmed. "She stunned me by agreeing to it, but when it happens.... When London is gone— I don't know what will happen to her."

"She's family, so we'll help her. All of us," Lissa offered.

"I don't know how receptive she'll be to that or if your mom would even want that."

"My mom will want to help her, even though she hurt her. That's how she is."

"Yeah, I can see she has a big heart. That's how London was too. Why can't I?"

"What do you mean?"

"My girlfriend broke up with me today," he said. "Because I didn't care enough about her. How can I care so much about my patients and let my own relationship just die?"

She frowned as she considered what to say.

"The hell am I doing? You're thirteen. This conversation is way too heavy for you."

"Is not!" She scoffed. "Ugh, I hate thirteen. It's always, you're not old enough, but then also you're old enough to know better."

"It's not a fun age," Gus agreed. "Still, I can't be venting to you about all this. It's too much."

"I'm almost fourteen anyway, and I do sort of understand girlfriends and boyfriends and all that. But—"

"But what?"

"Don't tell anyone; I haven't told anyone yet." She turned to make sure no one was standing in the doorway.

"Tell anyone what?"

"I don't like... um, I think I like girls." She felt her cheeks flushing as she confessed it.

"Oh," his eyebrows raised in surprise, but then he gave her a gentle smile. "It's okay; you don't have to be embarrassed about that."

His face was honest and genuine and suddenly this enormous thing she'd been holding in didn't seem so big and bad anymore. Her nerves eased up as she let out a breath. "I just...guys are so gross, but I don't know, I'm kind of confused. I was going to talk to my Aunt Carly cause she's really cool, but then all this stuff happened with Loni."

"Well, I'm honored that you talked to me. If you like girls, that's okay, it doesn't change who you are, it just becomes another layer of you. And if you're not sure that's okay too; it's all part of growing up. People are fluid, always changing and growing, we don't stay the same, but discovering who you are, and what you want is what life is all about. Don't ever be embarrassed by it."

"Do you think my mom and dad would be okay with it?"

"From what I know about them so far, I do, yeah. You got a good family; they're going to support you."

"I don't want to dump it on them now with Loni and stuff."

"Your mom let me vent about Jenny one night. She said the distraction from thinking about Loni helped her a little."

"She did?"

"She did, and she's always worried about you," Gus said. "The last thing she wants is you feeling like you can't go to her right now. She'll welcome a talk with you. I know she will."

"I don't know..." she said nervously.

"I thought you were a fearless ninja girl? Do I have to take the nickname back?"

"Don't you dare!" She jumped up and did a spin kick in the air. "Or I'll show you how ninja-like I can be."

"Careful my face is too pretty for bruises," he ducked out of the way.

She giggled at that as she flopped back down in her chair.

"You're crazy if you don't think you have a big heart like my mom and your sister," Lissa told him, her chest tightening with emotion. "I was so scared to tell anyone that and you made me feel so much better."

"But—"

"But nothing. Plus if you didn't care about your girlfriend, why you crying?"

"Guilt mostly. I hate that I broke her heart," he confessed. "I hate that the only way I could fix it, would be a lie. I don't want to be with her. So she just has to be hurt and it just has to be my fault."

"I do understand that! It's kind of like when I know I shouldn't do something, but do it anyway," she mused. "My dad and mom get disappointed in me and I feel bad. But—I can't help myself sometimes."

"Not following your train of thought there, Ninja Girl."

"Okay so it's not exactly the same but the bad feeling is, I guess. It'll go away though. It always does for me, usually as soon as I'm done being grounded."'

He tilted his head back and laughed heartily. "You sound like me when I was kid. I was always acting out, and London was perfect making me seem even worse."

"Yeah we're twins," Lissa agreed. "So same. I can't see you being a bad kid though."

"I stopped acting out when I realized I wanted to be a doctor like my dad," Gus explained. "Turns out I just needed something to focus on."

"Huh," she mumbled. "Maybe that's what I need to."

"Do you know what you do when you grow up?"

"I never thought about it," she mused. "But I sure like watching all you doctors running around like crazy. Maybe I'll be a doctor."

"If you do decide to do that, I'll help you."

"Really?"

"Of course, that's what uncles are for."

"Thanks," she stood and held her arms out and he looked at her funny.

"You got a lot to learn about our family, Uncle Gus, we're huggers," Lissa said firmly. "Now get over here!"

He shook his head with a chuckle but stood to embrace her. She felt a hundred times better than she had earlier. Like a whole weight came off her shoulders.

Suddenly she wasn't so scared to talk to her mom anymore.

Chapter 17

As the days turned into a week, Loni was making a full and speedy recovery from her surgery, and the doctors were happy with her progress. She was getting an hour once each day to be off her machines, and they did a little something different with the time every day.

One day they had lunch in the cafeteria; it was amazing to sit at a table and eat again, even better with other people to talk with, even if it was just her parents. On another day, Carly had brought Loni an armload of cute pajamas to choose from, and she got to 'shop' from the waiting lounge.

Today Loni was with Lissa, who wheeled her into the elevator amid her parents' warnings to be careful.

"We're in a hospital!" Lissa reminded them as the elevator door closed.

"I thought the surgical wing was the top floor; that's twelve," Loni mentioned as Lissa hit a button to go up to level thirteen.

"It is for patients." Lissa grinned. "Wait till you see this."

The elevator beeped, and Lissa wheeled them off it. Loni noticed it was only lit with the emergency lights.

"I don't think we're supposed to be up here."

"I do it all the time." Lissa wheeled her down the long and empty corridor, and Loni noticed this area was all just a bunch of rooms, no lobby or receptionist area as the cardiology wing had.

"Most of the rooms are locked," Lissa explained as they continued. "This used to be a training area because this was a teaching hospital. Well, it still is, but not like it used to be. They used to have a large group of doctors here training and learning. Now they only have a few, so most of these rooms aren't needed."

"How do you know all this?"

"Uncle Gus," Lissa said as she wheeled Loni into an open room. She switched the light on, and the bright fluorescent light quickly highlighted the large classroom-style room with several small lab areas set up.

"Is that a person!" Loni gasped and then felt foolish as she looked closer at the naked man lying on a table in front of the classroom. It sure looked real at first glance.

"This is super cool. It's called a syndaver. It's a replica of the human body for doctors to practice." Lissa looked all excited as she wheeled Loni closer to it. "It has all the organs in it and everything!"

"It's freaking me out!" Loni squealed, turning her face away.

"Such a scaredy cat," Lissa teased. She stood in front of the dummy and started to reach towards it.

"Don't touch it!"

"I already have!" Lissa said gleefully. "It's not liked they're real, but they used to use real cadavers here; know what that is?"

"Does it matter if I want to know?" Loni rolled her eyes. "You're going to tell me anyway."

"Real human bodies!" She said so full of excitement over it that Loni seriously questioned her little sister's sanity.

"What do you mean, real humans?"

"Well, dead, obviously," Lissa scoffed. "They've been doing that for years. They don't do as much teaching now, so they got the fake ones. This one is already opened because they demonstrated open heart surgery last week."

Loni gaped as Lissa pulled apart the 'chest' and stuck her hand in there; she then pulled out a replica of a human heart and held it up. Loni shuddered as Lissa's eyes lit up further.

"Did Gus tell you all this?"

"Yeah, he showed me too," Lissa nodded. "What they'll do during the surgery, I mean."

"He did?"

"I was a little scared, so he walked me through it. When he did, it didn't seem as scary anymore. It's a procedure with steps to follow, just like when dad cooks something, he follows a recipe."

"That is not even close to the same thing."

"In a way, it is. You follow the directions, one step at a time. The more you do, the better you are, and John is the best. You're going to be okay."

"I hope so," Loni sighed, frowning lightly; she'd been trying to keep her mind off it, but that was easier said than done. John was so impressed with how quickly she was healing from the surgery he'd scheduled for her heart replacement for the end of the week, just four more days. London would be transferred in just two days.

"I know so!" Lissa was still holding the heart replica.

"Will you put that thing back? It's freaking me out?"

"Fine, but I think it's cool. I might even be a doctor like Uncle Gus someday."

"Really?" Loni perked up at that. "You've never talked about what you want to be when you grow up."

"I never really thought about it, but I like walking around here, watching the doctors."

"Really?"

"Yeah, they all have so much purpose and rush."

"They do all have a certain high-energy kind of thing, and that is you for sure," Loni agreed.

"I hung out in the hall and watched them training here. I even shadowed the pediatrician on her rounds yesterday." Lissa looked very excited, and Loni was soon grinning along with her.

"You did what?" Luca's voice interrupted the sister's chat, and they looked up to see him and Kit walking into the room.

"How'd you know we were up here?" Lissa asked.

"Gus told us this is your new favorite spot," Kit explained. "Lissa, you can't be getting in the way of the doctors here."

"I wasn't!" Lissa protested. "I was having breakfast with Uncle Gus and her in the cafeteria, and he told her I was thinking about being a doctor and she offered. The kids loved me."

"A doctor, huh?" Luca smirked as a flash of pride flickered in his eyes.

"Our little doctor, I could see her in the scrubs now," Kit gushed as she played with Lissa's hair, who made a face and shooed her away.

"But," Luca said in a firmer tone. "You got to be better in school. Doctors need to have good grades, to get into a good college."

"I know they all warned me of that," Lissa said. "I'm going to work harder in school next year."

"They all?" Kit questioned.

"I'm getting pretty popular among the staff here," Lissa said. "If you need any gossip, I'm your girl."

"Don't tell your aunt Carly that she'll have you talking for hours," Kit advised.

Luca just shook his head and sighed.

"What's wrong, Dad?" Lissa asked curiously.

"Dating, college, careers. I'm not ready for all this; you're just kids."

"We're teens, sorry, Dad," Loni smiled as Kit comforted his arm.

"They had to start growing up at some point, babe," Kit said, smiling sadly as she curled into his side.

"But why?" Luca whined.

"To torture you, Dad, obviously," Lissa scoffed.

"Well, it's working," he shot back." No boys, yet Shorty, please. I can't take anymore."

"Oh, uh... yeah." Lissa looked uncomfortable as she shifted from foot to foot, her eyes dropping to the ground.

"Lissa?" Loni asked worriedly. "You, okay?"

"Uh yeah, forget it," Lissa's face could never hide when she was embarrassed or upset, though, and it was very red. Loni frowned, wondering what made her suddenly flustered, and then it dawned on her as she took in what her dad had said. She'd been suspecting something like this for a while and wanted to have a heart-to-heart with Lissa before she ended up in the hospital.

"Lissa, it's okay," Loni said quickly.

"What's wrong, Hon?" Kit asked, and as she stepped closer, Lissa took a step back, reaching behind her for Loni s hand. Loni grabbed it and squeezed it tight to give her little sister courage.

"Shorty? What's up?" Luca sounded concerned.

"Um, just the guy thing..."

"Your dad was kidding. We know you don't like boys yet," Kit assured her, but a shadow of worry crossed her face. "Do you?"

"Of course, she doesn't. She's too young for—"

"Stop!" Loni spoke up for Lissa. "She's trying to tell you something, so let her talk."

Lissa squeezed her hand tighter and took a breath.

"So," Lissa said slowly. "First off, there isn't anyone I like in that way yet, probably not for a while. But. When- "

She stopped again, and her dad's worried gaze intensified; it wasn't like Lissa to be tongue-tied. Loni squeezed her hand tighter. "Go ahead, you got this," Loni encouraged her.

"When I am ready to date, I don't think I will be dating boys, so I don't think you'll have to worry about that, Daddio," Lissa said hurriedly; she then attempted a laugh, but it turned into a sob.

A flash of surprise passed over Luca's face as Kit's eyes softened in a loving but worried gaze, she quickly pulled Lissa from Loni into her embrace and Lissa buried her face against Kit s shoulder.

"It's okay, don't cry, please don't cry," Kit soothed and held her tightly to her. "We love you so much. I know it's hard being your age and going through this, but learning these things about yourself is what makes you, you. You will always be our adorable little spitfire, and we'll always love you, no matter who you date. You don't have to cry or be sad to tell us."

"Hey, listen to your mom, Shorty. All that matters to us is whoever you girls date treat you right." Luca started to rub her back as he chimed in. "We are so proud of you for telling us you don't need to be upset."

"Lissa, I'm so proud of you for saying it," Loni offered as a teary Lissa pulled away from Kit, wiping her eyes as her reddened cheeks slowly faded to normal.

"You knew?" Lissa asked Loni. "How? I didn't even know until recently; I'm still kind of confused."

"Sisters have a way of knowing things." Loni smiled reassuringly, "And it's okay to be confused. I'm here anytime you need to talk."

"Shorty, you didn't think we'd be upset about this did you?" Luca asked.

"I don't know," she mumbled nervously. "No one in our family has ever been gay before . At least, I don't think, and Aunt Mary got so mad that one day when the two guys were kissing on TV."

"Your great Aunt Mary is very extreme in her beliefs," Luca explained. "That's on her, but I don't agree. As far as I see it, only God can judge someone's choices. I might be cocky, but I'm not God."

"Sweetie, I see it the same way as your dad. I don't believe God would be against any love because our ability to give and receive love is our greatest gift. Why would He limit it?"

"Yeah! Why would He?" Lissa was cheering up quickly.

"He wouldn't," Loni agreed with her mom and dad.

"Please know that we will never be upset with you for being honest with us," Kit said. "Not ever; that goes for both of you. Please never be afraid to come to us and tell us anything, okay? Please. I need you girls to know Dad, and I will always be a safe space for you both."

"I do. I know that now, Mom," Lissa said as Kit pulled her in for another hug.

"Good," Kit kissed the top of her head. "I'm so proud of you for telling us."

"Thanks, Mom." She pulled away from Kit and walked over to Luca, who embraced her next.

"Listen to your mom, Shorty, we're pals; you can always come to me," Luca said as he ruffled her hair.

"Thanks, Daddio." She was nearly glowing with relief and Loni was so happy for Lissa at that moment she forgot all about her problems.

"We better get Loni back to the room before the docs come looking for her," Luca said, reminding her just like thar, and she sighed.

"Hours up just like Cinderella," Loni whined. "Expect I have to return the wheels instead of the glass slippers."

"For now, Pumpkin," Luca offered. "You won't need those wheels much longer."

Later that afternoon, Kit was with Luca and Lissa in Loni's room. Loni had fallen asleep some time ago. Luca was watching Wheel of Fortune with the volume off, Lissa was playing with her phone, and Kit was attempting to read the same book she'd been reading since Loni was admitted. She was only on page three.

Kit looked over at Lissa, who was typing something into her phone, probably texting a friend; she was still surprised by Lissa's admission but so proud of her for telling them. She hadn't suspected it herself, but Lissa had just started acting more mature over the last year or so.

"Mom?" Lissa looked up.

"Sorry, Hon, didn't mean to stare; who are you texting? Your little fingers are working overtime."

"Betsy, I had to fill her in on so much, we haven't talked in forever."

Betsy was Lissa's best friend since they met in first grade during roll call when they realized they were both named Elisabeth.

"I sent her that selfie we took with Loni and Uncle Gus, and she said Gus is cute." Lissa pulled a face at that, and Kit laughed softly.

"Nice to see you are bonding with your uncle so much," Kit commented.

"Yeah, I like him," Lissa agreed. "Mom, speaking of Uncle Gus, I better tell you something."

'What?" Kit furrowed her eyebrows.

"He told me he's worried about his mom, like super worried," Lissa said with a face full of concern. "He doesn't know what will happen to her after all this."

"I... see," Kit bit at her lip as her gut tightened into a knot.

"I mean, I know... things are weird, but she is your mom and my grandma, so I told him we'd help her," Lissa confessed. "I hope that's okay?"

"Lissa, I don't know about that," Kit said quietly. "I'm grateful to her, beyond grateful, but I still have a lot of feelings I haven't resolved and- "

"Then maybe it's time to do that, baby," Luca said.

"How?" Kit asked. "Where do I even begin?"

"Why not start with why and see where it takes you."

"I asked her why once and didn't believe her answer."

"Well, you're older now, and so is she," Luca said. "Look, people suck. They make crappy choices and hurt us, sometimes badly, and it's unfair. But no one should be defined by their biggest mistake. Because that's not fair either."

Of course, her mind went right to Leo, Luca's father, who was an extraordinary man in his final days. Had he been defined by his greatest mistake, it would have been a travesty. Luca was right, but that didn't make it any easier.

"Don't forgive her for her, do it for you," he added after a silent moment.

That brought a smile to her lips. "That sounds like good advice."

"It is. The smartest, sweetest, strongest, and most beautiful woman in the world gave me that advice once." He walked over towards her and pulled her up and into his embrace.

"Oh gag. You guys are so gross," Lissa groaned.

"Just wait, you'll be all gross and mushy someday, too," Kit teased, and she cringed.

"No way, never."

"Famous last words," Luca chuckled.

Chapter 18

"The hell is Salmon Oscar?" Stone was heading out into the hospital parking lot with his cell tucked between his chin and ear as he unlocked his truck. "Sorry, didn't mean to say Hell. What if we had that healthy pizza thing again?... Yeah, flatbread. I kind of liked that. ... Fine. Just text me what to pick up."

As he hung up the phone, he heard an all too familiar scoff and turned around to face Stacey leaning against a red car, having a smoke. "Are you telling me someone has Sutton Hart eating healthy?"

Stone cringed at his given name as he turned and met Stacey's gaze; her eyes were puffy and tired, and it was impossible to feel anything but empathy for her.

"Loni and her heart and all... Ava thinks I should balance better," Stone explained hastily.

"If you found someone you'll listen to, you better hold on," Stacey advised.

"It's not like that," Stone was gripping the handle of his truck uncomfortably, desperately wanting to escape the conversation.

"You just apologized for swearing," Stacey gave him a pointed look.

"I ain't talking about this with you, of all people."

"I deserve that."

"What's done is done."

"I wasn't in a good place then. My head wasn't right. It's not an excuse but a reason, I guess."

"I'm not the one you need to talk to about that."

"You would be one of the two people I should talk to about that," she countered.

"I'm not mad at you now, Stacey," Stone shrugged. "You were a kid, and so was I. Kit and I got by, and we got a tight bond. I don't care about me. Make things right with her."

"I'd like to," Stacey's voice dropped. "But is it possible?"

"Yeah, our girls got a big heart."

The long day of waiting was making Kit antsy, so she left the cafeteria and headed toward the parking lot for some air. Just as she pushed the big doors open and walked out, Stacey, smelling heavily of cigarette smoke, was about to walk in.

The older woman took a step back almost as if on instinct, and it took everything in Kit not to turn and run around inside. Instead, she stood still, facing the woman she'd cried so many tears over as a child, and harbored so much anger for as a teen, until finally, as an adult, she reached indifference.

How could she tear open old wounds now? But as she stood there and her eyes met the reddened and broken ones of her mother's, the better question was, how could she not?

"You're here already?" Kit questioned. "Is she?"

"Not yet," Stacey spoke quietly. "They're preparing her for transfer; moving a comatose patient is slow."

"Yeah, I can imagine it is."

There was an awkward moment as they fell silent, Kit ran a hand through her hair as Stacey shifted to her feet.

"I just saw your dad," Stacey broke the silence. "He looks good."

"For how much weed he smokes and beer he drinks, he's surprisingly spry," Kit agreed with a short chuckle.

"Well, his new girlfriend has him eating healthy that's a shocking start for him."

"Wait, what?" Kit's eyes shot wide open. "Girlfriend?"

"I heard him talking to an Ava about salmon and flatbread."

"Oh, Ava's not his girlfriend," Kit smiled as realization set in. "That's Loni's boyfriend's mom. They're staying with him for a while."

"You sure?" Stacey asked. "He apologized for cursing and got all funny when I asked him about it."

"I mean... she does seem good for him," Kit mumbled thoughtfully. Was Stone finally ready to settle down all these years later?

"Seems you were, too," Stacey commented. "He said you two had a tight bond."

"Yeah, we did," Kit looked down at her feet as she gulped. ".... Should we talk?"

"I'd like to," Stacey agreed quickly.

A group of doctors came bursting out the doors in a hurry whizzing past the two women as they darted off through the parking lot.

"Should we go inside?" Kit suggested, and Stacey nodded silently, letting Kit lead the way. She ducked down a corridor on the first floor, and Stacey followed.

"This was supposed to be a research wing," Kit explained as they walked down a short hall to an open lounge area with a few vending machines, leather couches, and chairs. It was more causally set up than the patient lounges. Surrounding the break area were several closed doors to various unused labs.

"It's not now?" Stacey asked as the women sat down.

"I guess they don't have the funding anymore," Kit explained. "That's what Gus was saying."

"That's a shame," Stacey commented.

"Yeah," Kit agreed. "I'm relieved they have a good cardiology department, though."

"This whole thing...must be such a nightmare for you."

"A waking nightmare." Kit nodded. "You know something about that."

"Six years," Stacey sighed wistfully, her soft brown eyes swimming with pain and longing.

"I don't know how to express my gratitude," Kit said as she gulped back her emotions. "There aren't even words, honestly. I just... thank you."

"I'm not the one to thank," Stacey confessed. "I didn't intend ever to let her go, but..."

"But...?"

"You can have me committed after this if you want, but here goes," Stacey breathed. "Sometimes, she speaks to me in her own way. I... sit with her and look at the flowers on the walls she painted every year. It brings me back there, and I'll remember being there with her, and I'll let myself dream so vividly about it and for that moment, I have her back."

Kit felt that lump in her throat grow bigger as she listened quietly, clasping her hands in her lap.

"But there are times, more so lately, when she will say something, she didn't say then. I think that's her way of getting messages to me now." Stacey continued. "Right before you entered her room, she had just told me it was time to let her go. Later when I heard you say your daughter dreamed about London's flower field, I knew. This is what London wants."

"I believe that," Kit whispered as her eyes started to burn with tears. "I knew that dream meant something. I know my sister is with Loni in her way too."

"She said she didn't need me anymore, but they do, meaning you and Gus, I think," Stacey let out a short humorous laugh. "No one needs me, or ever did, London included."

"That's not true," Kit cut her off. "I did need you."

"Cricket—"

"It's Kit," she snapped and then breathed to calm herself. "You said we can talk; I need to say this."

"Please, go ahead."

"When I was a little and all my friends had mamas, and I didn't, I needed you. I needed you When I laid in bed at night trying to remember what you looked like. When I went to my first day of school with lopsided pigtails and got picked on, I needed you."

Stacey let out a sob, but Kit took a breath and continued.

"That wasn't even the worst of that day. I spent the entire day being called a bug. Role call, the moment the teacher called out Cricket Hart, every kid in that room laughed. I got home in tears and told Dad. You know what he said?"

"What?" Stacey whispered.

"He said, toughen up, girl, let them laugh and show them you don't care. You decide who you're going to be, not a bunch of little brats." Kit smiled through teary eyes at the old advice. "That was the day I realized; I was okay. Did I still need a mom, yeah. But Stone and I had it. I decided I was Kit from then on out, and if anyone called me Cricket, I'd laugh before they could, and say, don't call me a bug's name."

".... But the thing is even still I didn't stop needing you. As I got older, the school was always doing stuff, like mother/daughter baking sales, or mom's volunteering for field trips, tea parties... I had to work hard to pretend I didn't care, but I did. I wanted to sign up for girl scouts so bad, but I knew it would be a constant reminder. I was angry with you during those years, Stacey. Really angry."

"You had every right to be," she whispered.

"As a young adult my focus shifted," Kit continued. "Luca's family took precedence, and then our life began, but I still needed you. On my wedding day, on the days I gave birth to my babies. And now- when one of them is bravely finding her way and the other is so sick and damn it I STILL need you."

With that Kit burst into tears and suddenly Stacey wrapped her arms around her and began to sob as well, they sat like that, for who knows how long simply sobbing. Kit didn't embrace Stacey back, but feeling her mother's arms around her after all these years did bring her an unexpected warmth.

"I'm sorry, I'm so sorry," she whispered the words fiercely. "I am here now, and I know it's too late but I am."

Kit pulled away wiping at her tear cheeks with her sleeve. "Was it true? The stuff about the drinking and the knife?"

"It was all true," Stacey said solemnly. "That and more. I was a wreck, Cri- Kit. I should have told Stone what was happening but I hid it well. Gus thinks it may have been postpartum depression; I believe he may be right looking back now."

"But you didn't have that with Gus or London?" Kit asked.

"To be honest, with Gus there was a touch of what I felt with you, but it only lasted a few weeks and was never to the extreme I had with you. It was like a disconnect with you, like – I loved you so much, but I didn't feel like I could connect with you or that I was good enough for you. I felt like you hated me."

Kit frowned as she quietly listened; Luca was right. Being older., and less angry made it easier to hear Stacey out.

"That coupled with us being in this tiny house in this town where I didn't know anyone. I felt so suffocated," Stacey added.

"But Dad said you were the one that wanted to move away."

"I was; I needed to get away from my parents," Stacey's eyes dimmed. "I didn't realize how closed in I would feel until I did, but I left because I had to. If I stayed there my neglect would have hurt you."

"I believe you," Kit whispered. "I forgive you for leaving because, as a mom, I understand protecting our babies even if we have to protect them from ourselves."

"Thank you... But, you don't have to do that; I don't deserve forgiveness."

"Wait," Kit stopped her. "I forgive you for leaving. But not for staying gone. I want I try and find a way though, so I can... Why? Why didn't you come back?"

"There is no good answer for that," Stacey sighed. "For a while I was in a dark place and drinking heavily. I got arrested and ended up in rehab. I did want to see you when I got out, but I was so scared. What if it was the same? What if that feeling of you hating me came back? What if it sent me right back down into that horrible place again? So, I didn't go and didn't go. I spent all day thinking about it and not doing it."

She paused for a moment, and Kit remained quiet.

"Finally, I had to move forward. I couldn't stay with my parents for another day. I got an office job and an apartment to maintain, and it started to fill my days."

"They never asked about me or wanted to see me?" Kit asked, and Stacey's eyes filled with deep-rooted pain.

"My mother did, but she didn't dare voice it," Stacey said softly. "My father was not a good man; he was livid I got pregnant out of wedlock and refused to allow us to speak of you. I tried to get her to leave with me both times I left. She wouldn't."

Kit reached over and took her hand, squeezing it. "Is she gone now?"

"Yeah," Stacey whispered. "For some time now. As is he."

"I'm sorry you lost her," Kit said gently. "And I'm sorry for whatever your father put you through. If you ever want to talk about that I would listen."

"Thank you for that," Stacey gulped. "I have shut that box though."

"Okay," Kit squeezed her hand.

They took a silent moment, a peaceful calm washing over them despite the intense conversation.

"I was out to lunch one day when I met Jonathan. We bonded fast, and the next thing I knew we were dating, then engaged, and then married, and I just- never told him, and soon it just became this huge secret, I could never tell. This big shameful thing. Not you. Never you; I was ashamed of what I did." Stacey stopped to blow her nose and then took a breath to continue. "I never stopped thinking about you. London looked so much like you; it made me cry at times. I thought about you daily and never forgave myself for what I did. I don't expect you to either; I mean it, I don't deserve it."

"The thing about forgiving someone is it's not just for that person; it's your yourself too," Kit said. "Holding ill feelings for people, isn't good for the soul, and I want to forgive you. It might take some time, but I want to."

She found she truly meant it, not just because of what Stacey was doing for Loni but for herself.

"I don't know what to say; your forgiveness isn't something I ever even considered possible," Stacey said softly. "It means everything."

"Knowing all these things I didn't know before is helping me understand where you were coming from."

"I'm glad for that; I am."

"You said with Gus you felt a touch of what you did with me, but not with London?" Kit quizzed.

"I- yeah," Stacey looked sheepish. "I, like I said with Gus, there was a bit of disconnect, not like with you, but I was wishing for more of this magical connection I hear about, and it wasn't like that."

"You can't judge yourself based on what others experience," Kit offered.

"Hard not to compare," Stacey countered.

"Yeah, it is," Kit agreed.

"A part of me sometimes holds people at bay and closes off. Issues that stem from childhood, and I assumed it was from that. But then London was born."

Her eyes became misty again as she brought up her youngest.

"It was instant. I took one look at her, and her little unfocused eyes somehow looked right at me, and I thought, there she is, my very best friend. It was immediate the bond, the love; she took over my whole soul instantly. Her eyes were always full of adoration and love for me, pure, innocent love for her mama, and it just- It was incredible."

She took a long moment and then spoke again. "But I felt so guilty that I didn't have that with you or Gus. He knew I had a deeper bond with her, and it bugged him, yet I didn't try harder with him. There was this part of me that always knew, this deep fear, that I would lose her too soon, and maybe it was karma; I don't know, but I just knew."

"Mother's intuition," Kit offered.

"I guess so."

"I didn't have that for Loni," Kit's voice broke. "They said she'd been probably sick a month and I didn't know."

"Do not blame yourself; moms aren't super women, I know we're supposed to be, but we're not. We're just people, and we make mistakes, sometimes terrible ones."

Kit took a shaky breath as she nodded in agreement.

"If I could go back- "

"We can't go back," Kit cut her off. "It's pointless to sit here going over what-ifs. Especially now that we know how short life is. Let's move forward, me, you, and Gus. We'll get through it. Okay? Let's start now it's not too late."

"I'd be nothing but a burden to you and Gus; you don't need me."

"Knock it off; I just told you I need you," Kit scolded, albeit in a more playful tone. "And trust me when I say Gus needs lots of help. He's considering giving up on relationships."

"What?" Stacey balked. "He's twenty-six!"

"I know," Kit offered a half smile. "See. He needs us."

"I don't know what I'll be like; it's going to break what's already broken even more and..." Stacey trailed off.

"I know." Kit took her hand and held it tightly. "We will be there for you. For each other, we're all going to need each other."

"Yeah," Stacey offered a sad smile. "We are."

Chapter 19

"So put on your best boys and I'll wear my pearls."

"Loni?"

Loni woke up with a slight yawn as Manny gently squeezed her hand.

"Manny?" She smiled slightly. "When did you get here?"

"A little while ago," he brushed her hair back from her face. "How are you feeling?"

"Honestly? I'm exhausted; that started again this morning," Loni said as she yawned. "The doctors say the Brugada is flaring up again."

"I overheard them whispering about it," Manny admitted. "I think they're going to move your surgery up."

"I figured that might happen," Loni confessed. "John warned me."

"I think they're all getting ready for London to arrive, and your dad and Lissa had to make a quick run to your house," Manny was standing as he talked; he stepped to the corner of her room and grabbed her wheelchair, wheeling it over to her.

"What are you doing?" Loni asked as he brought it closer.

"Your uncle disconnected you already. We have about twenty minutes, and then I have to take you to London's room when she arrives." He helped a bewildered Loni into her wheelchair.

"Where are we going?"

"Not far." He wheeled her through the cafeteria into a little corridor and then into a room that looked like an empty lab. However, the table had a huge bouquet of flowers and a portable radio next to it. The room was lit with some fake LED candles, all flickering and giving it romantic lighting. He walked over and turned the radio on, and a soft love song started to play. She sat in her chair, staring up at him with teary eyes.

"You did all this?"

"Your dad and Gus helped me a little," he confessed. "I didn't want to wait another second for our first date, even if it has to be short."

"This is amazing!"

"May I have this dance?" He held his hands out, and she clasped them in hers.

She giggled as he began to spin her wheelchair around, her eyes locking onto his warm ones as they smiled gently at each other.

"Manny, I want to stand up and dance with you," Loni said, and his gaze faltered.

"I don't know, if anything happens..."

"Just for a minute," she pleaded. "I want to be in your arms, just once, just in case it's our only chance."

He sighed but still pulled her to her feet. She wobbled at first, but Manny wrapped his arms securely around her and pulled her up flush against him; she wrapped her arms around his neck and rested her head on his shoulder. They didn't sway or move to the music; they stood there and held each other.

"Don't say it'll be our only chance," he murmured. "It can't be. You have to fight, Loni. You have to get through this."

She sniffled as she pulled back from him, and their eyes locked.

"What if I don't?"

"You will," he stressed with a trembling voice. "You hear me? You have to!"

"But there's always a chance I might not, so you should prepare yourself for that; we should say goodbye just in case-"

"No," he cried. "I won't say it. I won't say goodbye to you. You will get through this. That's it."

"Oh, Manny." She half laughed and half sobbed out the words.

"I love you, Loni."

She gasped, her eyes welling with tears. "You... do?"

"Yeah, I do, and maybe someday you could love me too, so please fight for me, please?"

"Manny! I already do. I love you."

His green eyes lit up in a way she had never seen before, and she felt like she could float up to the sky as she lost herself in that gaze. She wasn't sure who leaned in first, and it didn't matter because the moment his lips touched hers, the entire world disappeared.

His lips were so soft as they moved slowly and tentatively against hers. The arm wrapped around her waist tightened, and she felt so secure and safe; her lips parted, and he deepened the kiss as Loni felt her body become weightless.

They were both flushed in the cheeks and breathless when they parted; a slow smile spread over his face. She was just about to lean in again when she heard her name being called from out in the cafeteria, and just like that, their tiny bit of time had come to an end.

They shared a sad smile as he helped her back into the wheelchair and started wheeling her to the door.

"Manny?" She said after a silent moment.

"Yeah, Loni?"

"I'm going to fight."

As Manny wheeled Loni out to the cafeteria, they found Gus, Lissa, and Luca waiting for them.

Gus nodded to follow him, and they did. Manny stepped away, and Luca took control of Loni's wheelchair as they headed down a new corridor.

All the doors were closed except one, a room her mom was standing outside of.

She's in there?" Loni asked hesitantly.

"Yeah. Listen, Honey," Kit said quietly. "John's worried this flare-up will get worse. He wants to operate tonight."

Loni gulped. "I had a feeling."

"It's going to be okay, Pumpkin." Luca squeezed her shoulders gently. "We're all here praying for you. You got this."

"Yeah," Loni whispered bravely.

"Why don't you go in and see her? Stacey said to have you come in first. She's in there with her now."

Loni gulped and wheeled herself to the open room. Her eyes widened at how much the woman on the bed looked like her mom. The older woman that had visited her before was sitting next to London.

"Hi, Leondra," she smiled sadly. "It's almost time."

"She's so beautiful," Loni said as she wheeled closer.

"She is," Stacey agreed.

"I want to thank you for giving me that sketch. It did inspire me."

Loni reached into her robe pocket and pulled out a folded piece of paper. She handed it over to Stacey, whose face lit up as she opened it. "This is so incredible!"

"I loved how she blurred all the flowers she'd ever seen into one, so I took that concept but made it into the shape of a heart," Loni explained. "The heart of London."

"This is so perfect so her." Stacey wiped a tear from her eye. "You're letting me keep this?"

"Yes, please," Loni said. "I want you to have it. I took a photo of it with my phone. I'm going to have it tattooed on me after all this."

"That's a beautiful idea," Stacey mused as she looked at the paper.

"I have to talk my mom into it first thought,"Loni admitted with a short laugh.

"I'll see if I can help with that," Stacey offered. "I'm going to give you a moment alone with her."

Loni nodded as Stacey sniffled and left, shutting the door behind her.

"Thank you," Loni spoke to London softly. "For giving me this chance to live. I'm going to do it for both of us. I'm going to follow both of our dreams. I'm going to laugh twice as much and love even harder. I'm going to make you proud that I have your heart."

"But I think you're most worried about your mom, huh?" Loni sighed softly. "I know I would be; I'll watch out for her, okay? I promise."

There was a knock at the door, and she looked up as John, Gus, Stacey, and the others walked back in.

"Is it time?" Loni asked.

"Your parents and sister will bring you to the surgery unit, and the nurses will prepare you. I'll be up soon after," John said, giving Loni's shoulder a light squeeze, "you got this, Loni."

She nodded bravely.

"I'm going to see you on the other side, Kid." Gus ruffled her hair, and she sniffled.

Kit wheeled her out of the room, and they were silent until they reached the elevator.

"I'm going to be okay," Loni promised her family. "I love you all too much to leave you. I'm going to get through this.

"Oh honey, we love you so much," Kit dropped, kissed her cheek, and Luca dropped in front of her.

"You got to fight like hell for us, okay, pumpkin? We need you," Luca insisted.

"I will. I promise I will."

The room was silent as Gus, John, and Stacey stood around London's bed.

"I wish - it didn't have to end like this," Gus stammered. "But at least now there was a reason at least now. She can live on. I miss you, London. It's so unfair that you didn't get your life. So damn unfair, but now you get peace."

He rested a hand on her cheek as a tear slipped down his cheek, "I love you, little sister."

"Oh, Little Red," Johnathan cried out. "I never understood why we only got you for such a short time. I never made sense of it; how was it fair that I saved so many lives and couldn't do a thing for you?"

"I can do this now, though. I can save your niece, and you can save so many others." He took her hand and squeezed it gently. "At least some good can come from tragedy."

He leaned down and kissed her cheek. "Love you, baby girl."

Stacey gulped as she took her place at London's side. Her constant place for so many years now.

"I don't know how to say goodbye to you," Stacey began. "I suppose that was always my problem. I couldn't let you go. I fought you growing up. I fought you about art school. And even now, I made you hold on not for you, but for me."

"My father was a selfish man. I never meant to be like him, but in some ways, I was. It's time now that I finally listen to you, Sweetheart. It's time I let you go, but I'll never for a single moment stop loving you."

Stacey kissed her forehead and then both her cheeks. Then finally, she pulled back and looked up at Gus and John.

"Go ahead," she said bravely. "I'll be right behind you."

John grabbed one end of the bed, and Gus held the other. Stacey followed behind them as they wheeled her from the room.

"The Ballad of a Dove. Go with peace and love."

The waiting room was full of people. Luca sat with Kit's hand in his and Lissa on his other side. Stone was next to Lissa with Ava and Manny on a couch.

Across from them sat Carly, Andre, and the twins. Kathy, Andrea, and a few other school kids took up the couch beside theirs.

And standing, pacing the room, was Stacey. Gus was often in and out with updates; he couldn't operate but could go that much.

After several hours Gus came out for an update, his eyes dimming as he reached Stacey.

"London is gone."

She clamped a hand over her mouth and sobbed. His caught her before she dropped to the floor; Kit shot up from her seat and joined Gus in holding Stacey up.

Stacey stayed even though Kit was sure she wanted to leave. She sat on the other side of Kit and held her hand, and the first step towards forgiveness was made.

Finally, after several hours, an exhausted-looking John and Dr. Morgan came down, Gus standing behind them.

Kit and Luca rose simultaneously as they took a step forward.

"She made it through the surgery." John didn't make them wait for it; Kit's entire body filled with relief, so much so she nearly fell had it not been for Luca holding her up. "Vitals are good, and she's not showing signs that she will reject the heart."

"Oh, thank God," Luca cried. This time Kit and Luca both did drop to their knees. They sat they're for a moment embracing before they stand back up.

"Can we see her?" Kit asked.

"Soon," Dr. Morgan said. "The nurses are bringing her into a recovery room. Once she is settled, I will come to get you."

"She did amazing." John offered a a warm smile.

"I don't know how we can ever thank you," Luca said.

"No need," John said.

"We should thank you instead," Stacey had walked over. "Because of your daughter, ours still got to make her mark on this world."

"Will you stay for a bit?" Kit asked. "Loni would like to see you when he wakes up."

"Of course, I will."

"Thanks, Mom."

Stacey teared up as she nodded and Gus took her arm to walk with her.

Kit looked at Luca with teary eyes who pulled her into his arms and she wrapped hers as tightly around him.

"Our girl's going to be okay," Luca cried as he kissed her head. "She's going to be okay."

"I knew she would, I always knew as scared as I got," Kit pulled back enough to look at his, resting her hands on his cheeks.

"Your love carried her through it, carried us all through this," Luca said.

"No all of our love did."

Epilogue

Four Weeks Later

"I'll put one hand in the air. I'm closing my eyes. My whole heart's beating for the first time. That boy here in town says, "Darlin', just drive. " I swear the gates of Heaven just opened up wide."

The mother stood in the center of the flower field; the colors seemed more vibrant this year than ever.

She plopped down amongst the purple wildflowers admiring the rose buses, two now.

"London, the roses are back." She spoke out of habit; she turned her head to the side, half expecting her little girl to be sitting beside her.

Instead, she heard a car in the distance and saw a little blue car slowing as it grew closer to the field.

"You're finally here."

The radio in the car was blaring, and the pretty young driver was singing and smiling, one hand in the air. Next to her sat that adorable boy who was so devoted to her.

She slowed and stopped the car, and he got out first, then ran over to open her door.

Good boy, she noted.

He handed the girl a box and she took it carefully into her arms. She kissed his cheek and whispered something in his ear, and he nodded, and sat back, waiting to give the two of them their moment.

She then turned and smiled as she walked toward the mother...

....well, grandmother, waiting for her in the field.

"Leondra! You're glowing! Are you feeling as good as you look?" Stacey asked as they drew closer to each other.

"Better every day," Loni was all smiles as she carefully handed off the box to Stacey. "Here she is."

Stacey took it and held it close to her. This wasn't how she imagined London returning to this special place, but she was glad she was here.

"Welcome back, Sweetheart," Stacey said out loud. "There are two rose bushes this year; we waited so long for the one to return, and now look."

She carefully set the box by the bushes as Loni approached to look closer.

"My gosh!"

"What is it?"

"It's a pink rose bush," Loni said. "That's my grandmother Elizabeth; we always felt like the pink rose was her sign. I think she and my grandpa are here to care for London on her way home."

"That's beautiful!" Stacey sobbed, and Loni quickly embraced her. They'd spent a lot of time together her since the surgery. She'd begun spending as much time at the hospital as Kit and her husband Luca. Leondra was finally released a week ago.

They stood for several moments in peaceful quiet, enjoying the field and feeling the presence of London.

"My mom let me, by the way, I'm guessing you helped?" Loni rolled up her sleeve to show her.

She'd tattooed the heart of London sketch on her inner wrist. Stacey lifted her own sleeve and showed Loni she'd gotten the same tattoo on her inner wrist as well.

"I told her how much I'd love for us both to have them and I knew she'd agree," Stacey smiled. "I think she may get one too."

"They look perfect," Loni said as they held the matching tattoos close and admired them.

More cars came and broke up the quiet moment.

"It's time." Loni said.

She waved and nodded to Manny, who started walking towards them carrying his guitar.

The other two cars parked, alongside the field. Johnathan and Gus climbed out of the first one. and Kit, Luca, and the adorable Lissa got out, of the second one. She, like her parents, insisted on her short name being used, so Stacey was getting used to that. Lissa, looked a lot like London and Kit with her red hair, but she reminded Stacey of a young Gus with her spunky attitude.

Stacey picked up the box and held it close to her as everyone approached.

"Ready, Mom?" Kit asked gently.

"I am," Stacey gulped.

They all began to walk through the field slowly as Manny started to play a lullaby on his guitar.

"Wait." Gus stopped him. "She'd want it to be a love song."

"Yeah," Stacey agreed. "She would."

"Now I know there's no such thing as enough time"

...And so Manny played a love song as Stacey opened the box that contained London's ashes. They all reached in to pull out a handful of ashes out and tossed them into the air. They begun to walk as they continued on. One handful after another until the box had been emptied and someone had taken it from her.

Stacey watched with misty eyes as what was left of her daughter was carried by the wind across the field of flowers she loved so much.

A hand took hers, and she looked at her older daughter Kit, who was offering a comforting smile. Her other hand than was also gently grasped, and she turned to see Gus on her other side.

"We got you, Mom," he offered. "We'll get through this."

"Look." Kit motioned ahead to where Loni was walking hand in hand with her boyfriend, a big bright smile on her young face. Like London's, her eyes were so pretty, a soft honey-brown. They were full of hope, love, dreams... life. They were full of life.

Her granddaughter now had time to bloom, and her daughter finally found peace.

Someday with the help of her children and grandchildren she would too.

"So put on your best boys and I'll wear my pearls."

Milton Keynes UK
Ingram Content Group UK Ltd.
UKHW021925151124
451262UK00014B/1612

9 781933 121529